The
BS
Situation of Tougetsu
Umidori

A second-year classroom in an ordinary high school. Sixth period had ended, and the students were all getting ready to go home—only the two of them were sitting still.

The first speaker was Yoshino Nara, a girl with short hair.

With her was Tougetsu Umidori, a girl with long hair.

"A thief!" Nara proclaimed.

"I've been robbed!"

"…………Huh?"

Bullshit-chan

A girl born from a lie. She appears
before Tougetsu Umidori and
requests her help eating other lies—
so that she might live.

"Ta-daa! *Omurice!*
I just made this! Heh-heh,
surprised? I'm actually
a great cook!"

"......Wh-what do I do, what do I do, what do I do? I'm eating eating eating out with a girl from class...!"

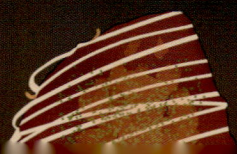

"Thank you for joining me today, Umidori," Nara said. She was using a metal spatula to split up the *modanyaki* on the grill in front of them.

1 The Pencil Incident —— 001

2 Bullshit-chan Holds Forth —— 035

3 The Girl Named Yoshino Nara —— 051

4 Young and Old, Male and Female —— 079

5 A Painful Defeat —— 095

6 Mud Hat —— 113

7 Showdown in a Children's Park —— 137

8 Tougetsu Umidori and Yoshino Nara —— 157

The BS Situation of Tougetsu Umidori

CONTENTS

Kaeru Ryouseirui

Illustration by
Natsuki Amashiro

1

The BS Situation of Tougetsu Umidori

YEN ON
New York

The
BS
Situation of Tougetsu Umidori

1

Kaeru Ryouseirui

Illustration by
Natsuki Amashiro

Translation by **Andrew Cunningham**

UMIDORI TOUGETSU NO 「DETARAME」 NA JIJOU Vol.1
©Kaeru Ryouseirui 2021
First published in Japan in 2021 by KADOKAWA CORPORATION, Tokyo.
English translation rights arranged with KADOKAWA CORPORATION, Tokyo through TUTTLE-MORI AGENCY, INC., Tokyo.

English translation © 2024 by Yen Press, LLC

Yen On
150 West 30th Street, 19th Floor
New York, NY 10001

Visit us at yenpress.com ❧ facebook.com/yenpress ❧ twitter.com/yenpress ❧ yenpress.tumblr.com ❧ instagram.com/yenpress

First Yen On Edition: December 2024
Edited by Yen On Editorial: Maya Deutsch
Designed by Yen Press Design: Andy Swist

Library of Congress Cataloging-in-Publication Data
Names: Ryouseirui, Kaeru, author. | Amashiro, Natsuki, illustrator. | Cunningham, Andrew, 1979- translator.
Title: The BS situation of Tougetsu Umidori / Kaeru Ryouseirui ; illustration by Natsuki Amashiro ; translated by Andrew Cunningham.
Other titles: Umidori tougetsu no "Detarame" na jijou. English
Description: New York : Yen On, 2024.
Identifiers: LCCN 2024039140 | ISBN 9781975390624 (v. 1 ; trade paperback) | ISBN 9781975390648 (v. 2 ; trade paperback) | ISBN 9781975390662 (v. 3 ; trade paperback) | ISBN 9798855407730 (v. 4 ; trade paperback)
Subjects: LCGFT: Fantasy fiction. | Light novels.
Classification: LCC PL880.3.Y68 U6513 2024 | DDC 895.63/6--dc23/eng/20240827
LC record available at https://lccn.loc.gov/2024039140

ISBNs: 978-1-9753-9062-4 (paperback)
        978-1-9753-9063-1 (ebook)

10 9 8 7 6 5 4 3 2 1

LSC-C

Printed in the United States of America

1

The Pencil Incident

"A thief!" Nara proclaimed. "I've been robbed!"

"............Huh?"

Umidori had been stuffing the contents of her desk into her bag but stopped in surprise, turning to Nara.

A second-year classroom in an ordinary high school.

Sixth period had ended, and the students were all getting ready to go home—only the two of them were sitting still.

The first speaker was Yoshino Nara, a girl with short hair.

With her was Tougetsu Umidori, a girl with long hair.

"...Um, a thief?" Umidori asked, setting her bag back down under her chair. "Where'd this come from? Are you missing something?"

"I'm not missing anything. It's been stolen!"

Nara pounced on her words, sounding despondent.

".......Th-that sounds serious. Your wallet? Phone?"

But Nara dismissed Umidori's concern.

"Neither. Nothing remotely like that. Someone has stolen *my pencil*."

"Um."

"My pencil has been pilfered!"

"..............Huh?"

Nara's pronouncement briefly silenced Umidori. Her cheeks quivered as she sat there, speechless—but in time, she managed a dubious frown.

"......H-hang on, what are you talking about, Nara? A stolen pencil? Do you mean your pencil's gone missing?"

"I do not, Umidori. It's not missing, it's stolen!"

Nara pounced on that statement once again, but this merely left Umidori scratching her cheek, befuddled.

".......I'm lost. Is this some sort of elaborate joke?"

"I am not joking in the slightest, Umidori. I have never been more serious."

Nara snorted, as if annoyed—but that was all. Her expression betrayed no such emotion. Not one muscle on her face moved perceptibly. She had *no* expression. It was as if her cheeks were coated in wax, rendered immobile.

Yoshino Nara. Reddish hair cut neatly around her neck. A delicate figure. A distant vibe.

"Hear me out, Umidori. I'm sure you've noticed I am a die-hard pencilhead. I would never dream of writing with something as unsoft as a *mechanical* pencil. That said, pencil lead is easily breakable, and once broken, there is little that can be done. To that end, I make sure my pencil case is perpetually fully stocked. I always keep exactly *five* pencils within.

"It's been like this since I was in grade school. I take care of my things—I might swap out the contents of the case at home, but I almost never misplace them. If we limit the scope to high school alone, I can confidently say I have *never* lost a single pencil."

However neutral her expression, her voice was hardly emotionless.

Nara's tone varied wildly, as if compensating for how rigid her features were. The words flowed free, rife with feelings. As if she could not bear to be silent.

".......Um, what?"

But the more Nara spoke, the deeper Umidori frowned.

"Nara, are you seriously insisting that someone must have stolen your pencil because you don't believe you could possibly have lost one?"

Tougetsu Umidori. Black hair all the way down her back. A gentleness to her eyes that made her seem approachable. She was quite tall for a second-year high school girl; even sitting down, her eyes were a full head higher than Nara's own.

"I-I'm not buying it. That's hardly logical. No matter how careful you might be, pencils get lost all the time through ordinary use. And you can buy all the pencils you want at the one-hundred-yen shop to begin with! Nobody's going to bother stealing one. They're just not in demand!"

"......All that is true." Nara nodded, accepting Umidori's reasoning. "You're not wrong, Umidori. I'm certainly careful to avoid misplacing them, but it's not like I've concocted some infallible plan. And yes—I have a massive stock of pencils back home. Losing one is of no consequence whatsoever. If I had merely *lost* a pencil, I would just think, *Oops*, and forget about the whole thing.

"The issue before us is not *what* was stolen—but *how*."

Nara pulled her pencil case out of the desk and began arranging the contents in a row.

"......Um, but you still have five?"

Umidori counted them off on her fingers. No mistaking that number.

"Exactly. I do indeed have five pencils—which is why I'm certain one was stolen."

"..............?"

"Begin by handling them yourself. This should tell you everything."

As prompted, Umidori selected one of the pencils and picked it up.

"Well?"

"......Nothing unusual about it. It's an ordinary pencil."

"Okay. Try the next one."

Baffled, Umidori did as told. She picked up a second pencil—and frowned.

"......That's odd. There's a slight...depression."

It was right around the middle of the pencil. So slight it wasn't visible to the naked eye—but now that the pencil was in her hand, she could clearly feel the dent in the side.

Umidori checked the remaining pencils. With the exception of the first she'd handled, each had a similar indentation. Each dent was in a different spot, but they were consistently so subtle they could only be identified by physically holding them.

"I made those indentations," Nara revealed, once Umidori had verified all five pencils. "I rapped each against something hard—after all, softness is a pencil's whole thing."

"......I don't know where you're going with this. You dented four, but not the fifth? Some sort of superstition in action?"

"That perspective muddies the waters. What if I told you I had made dents in all five of my pencils?"

"......Har?"

It took a Umidori a moment to figure that one out. Her head drifted to one side—and then she abruptly straightened up, her cheeks stiffening.

"You catch my drift, Umidori?"

Poker-faced, Nara let out a satisfied grunt.

"Last night, I doctored every pencil in my case. Denting each in a different spot, careful to ensure this was impossible to perceive without touching the pencil directly. I checked the dents again before first period began. Yet as you yourself noticed, for some reason, one of the dents has disappeared. Without a trace.

"Pencils have no self-repairing properties. Obviously! Therefore, this pencil is *not mine*. The brand, length, and sharpness of the lead—all identical to the original pencil. Yet it is an entirely different one. But where did the pencil I dented go? Why does my pencil case contain a pencil identical to my own, yet entirely different?"

Nara snatched up one of the pencils, running her finger along the depression.

"Someone swapped it out! Somebody stole one of my pencils and took pains to ensure I wouldn't notice. Matching not just the brand and length but the sharpness of the lead? That way lies madness. Someone who'd go that far has to be insane. But why did this unhinged thief swipe my pencil? Did they forget their pencil case at home? Clearly not! They're a freak! The freakiest of freaks!"

Nara's expression remained placid—but she was spitting her words, sounding utterly repulsed.

Umidori sat there stunned, her jaw hanging open.

"At first, something just felt vaguely *wrong*. A pencil I'd held but an hour ago felt somehow *different*. I couldn't possibly be specific. I assumed I must have been imagining things. This happened five times in the second half of last year, and I paid it no attention. Even if a freak like that existed, I assumed there was no way they could replace my pencil with one so similar I couldn't tell the difference."

"..............."

"Honestly, I was just curious. This whole idea was ludicrous, utterly impractical—but it wasn't physically *impossible*. Perhaps this freaka-zoid actually existed. And so, I decided to test the idea, just in case. I figured I could laugh about it with my friends later on. Acting like a hotshot detective, I laid a cunning trap. I knew the odds of the thief noticing were slim. This pilferer has taken downright unnatural pains to avoid discovery. They must be a terrifyingly cautious individual. But that also means they must be *bold* at the moment of the crime. If they dither at all, people will notice. I figured they'd have no opportunity to notice the marks I left."

Nara broke off, taking a deep breath. She was clearly wearing herself out—not that it showed on her face.

"I discovered the truth at lunch. I was flabbergasted. I have no words to describe just how horrified I was. This criminal scum—for the sake of brevity, let us call them the Pencil Thief—is flying their freak flag from the highest peak.

"It should go without saying, but just to be clear, this is no elaborate ruse I've concocted to mess with your head. I'll be honest—I do enjoy a good prank. But this is not one. I wish I was joking, but I'm afraid I am not. I may not show it, but I'm genuinely reeling here."

"..............! Wh-what in the......?!"

At last, Umidori's lips moved. All color had drained from her face. The facts that Nara had relayed to her must have come as a powerful shock.

"Er, so this Pencil Thief... Nara, you're saying someone in our class is behind this gross stalker move?"

"I'm afraid I must say the odds of that are high." Looking deeply bored, Nara let out a sad sigh. "I do not wish to suspect my classmates, but anyone capable of pulling off a crime of this complexity *must* be located within a degree of proximity to me. Close enough that they may well be listening in as we discuss the matter like this, heedless of who hears us."

Nara glanced around at the crowd of students getting ready to leave.

"That's actually...in part...the goal. I'm hoping to rattle the thief. They've been exceedingly careful, which means they're also a cow-ard. If they hear I'm onto them, it'll get under their skin. I hoped they would reveal themselves—but in reality, it seems everyone's so busy packing up they haven't heard a word I've said."

She shrugged and let out a sigh, her plans foiled. Umidori was scanning her surroundings, looking very twitchy, unable to settle down.

"The culprit is among us. That fact, that sinister truth has left me in a stupor since lunch. Only now that the day is over have I begun to settle down."

Umidori's eyes had not settled down at all, and Nara caught her gaze.

"I think the next step is to identify this Pencil Thief. And I'll need your help, Umidori."

"......Oh?"

"I mean, having some enigmatic stalker lurking in our vicinity is just unnerving, right? Now that I know they exist, I cannot stand idly by. Perhaps the theft of my pencils is the extent of the damage done, but that may not be true forever."

Nara let out a reluctant sigh.

"That said, going to the faculty at this stage would get me nowhere fast. They'd insist it's all in my head. We'll have to handle this ourselves. Pinpoint the criminal and demand they stop their freakish behavior. Honestly, it's an annoyance I could do without. Why should I have to bend over backward for some freaky freak?"

"...........Mm."

"To that end, I need a witness. Umidori, you sit next to me. Well? Did you see anyone acting suspicious around my desk at lunch today? Have you seen anyone with pencils like mine?"

"......Um."

Umidori rubbed her temples, considering the question. Choosing her words carefully.

"Sorry, Nara. I don't think I'll be much help. I didn't see who did it, and I haven't seen the stolen pencil since lunchtime."

"......Ah." Nara's shoulders slumped. "That's a shame. Well, I didn't think I'd nab them that easily."

"......But you do have a point, Nara. This does concern me."

Umidori nodded. The color had not returned to her face.

"Maybe this incident is no big deal, but the next case might be. We'll have to do something about it," she muttered. Her face was as grim as her voice. Clearly, she was doing her level best to think about the sinister incidents affecting her classmate.

"Heh-heh… I knew I was right to turn to you, Umidori."

"Oh?"

"You're the only friend I have who'd be this concerned about me. The pencil incident has nothing to do with you, yet here you are, as worried as if you were involved! I'm blessed to have a friend like you."

"………Nara," Umidori said, shifting awkwardly. "D-don't talk like that. I'm not that nice. I'm just a terrible liar, so you can read me like a book."

"Yes, I'm well aware. We haven't been friends a full year for nothing. You're the most honest, upstanding girl I know. One look at your face is enough to tell me everything on your mind."

Nara sounded like she was teasing, but this was high praise—even if her own expression might as well have been carved in stone.

Tougetsu Umidori was as expressive as Yoshino Nara was inexpressive. The two were polar opposites.

"If only you were willing to hang out more, you'd be the perfect friend. No matter how many times I invite you out, Umidori, you're never free. Like, how is it even possible for a high school girl to take that many shifts?!"

"……Ah-ha-ha. Sorry about that, Nara. The place I work never has enough staff to go around. It's dead busy all the time. I've gotta be at school on weekdays, so I do my best to work every weekend and holiday."

"Lord, you are such a pushover, Umidori. The shop may need help, but that's no reason to bend over backward! It's such a waste. You only get to be a high school girl once in your life, and you're wasting that whole time working.

"……Well, I guess I'm fine with that if you are. I have more than enough fun chatting with you in class."

But even as she spoke, Nara reached for Umidori's long hair, pulling it like she was trying to yank some out.

"Ow?! C-cut it out, Nara! What are you doing?"

"Heh-heh, once we leave, I won't see you till tomorrow. It's my last chance to savor those luscious black locks!

"Seriously, if I don't run my fingers through your hair at least four times a day, life isn't worth living. We shared a class all last year, too.

We've sat next to each other the entire time, too, so I've had the privilege of touching your hair on a daily basis. I can't see you on weekends—and I spend the whole time wistfully wishing I could wrap those locks around my fingers. It's like withdrawal."

"......! Y-you have the strangest sense of humor, Nara! My hair is hardly addictive. I know I've said this before!"

"Ha-ha! And it really shouldn't make you blush anymore. It's not like we only just got to know each other."

Nara might have been joking, but she also kept playing with Umidori's hair for quite a while. Only when she was thoroughly satisfied did she let the girl's tresses trail through her fingers.

"I've teased you enough. As for the Pencil Thief—we'll have to work on that. As long as we can solve the case before the end of April. I'm not about to spend my second high school Golden Week fretting about this creep."

"......R-right. Fair," Umidori said, straightening out the hair Nara had mussed. "Honestly, I'm not sure how much help I'll be, but you *have* been nice to me, and I'd like to help where I can when you're in trouble. If this Pencil Thief shows themselves to me, I'll slap them silly."

"Ha-ha! That would be a sight to see. If somewhat frightening. You're such a good friend. By the way, Umidori. Do you know what type of thief is the most fearless?"

Umidori considered that a moment but couldn't come up with anything.

"......? No, what kind?" she asked. "I've got no clue. What's the answer, Nara?"

"The kind who steals a cop car." Nara grinned.

Umidori had to admit that was truly fearless.

◇◇◇◇

Umidori made it home.

She pushed open the door to apartment 304, stepped through, and turned on the light switch as she took off her shoes. The sun hadn't set yet, but there were heavy curtains drawn over the windows; it was quite dark without the lights.

A simple kitchen and fridge sat just to the right of the entrance. To the left was the toilet, the bath, and the changing room in a row. Head straight through without turning, and the apartment featured a living room with a bed, a closet, and a round table—and basically nothing else. The window, set in the back wall, showed only the concrete surface of the building beyond; she basically never bothered opening the curtains.

Tougetsu Umidori resided in this studio apartment. She'd been living alone since spring of the previous year.

"......Whew."

Free of her shoes, she allowed herself a long sigh...and toppled over on the floor.

"Heh-heh... Ah-ha-ha-ha-ha-ha!"

Soon, she began to cackle maniacally.

"Ah-ha-ha-ha-ha! I was so stressed it nearly killed me!"

Flat on her back, she stuck a hand in her bag, rummaging around. Then she pulled something out—a paper bag the size of a dictionary, sealed with scotch tape. Umidori peeled off the tape and turned the bag upside down, letting the contents spill out.

Eyes on the falling pencils, Umidori broke out in an enraptured expression.

"......Oh, Nara! Nara! Naraaaa...!"

Clutching a handful of pencils, she chanted her classmate's name like one would a loved one.

"I never dreamed you would manage to get this far. You went our whole first year clueless, so I thought I was safe!"

Without bothering to sit up, Umidori began to slide herself along the floor.

"But if this was a test, Nara, you'd have failed! You only caught five out of a hundred!"

At this point, she reached the fridge.

"I'm only human. We all make mistakes. Perfection would be downright strange!"

Umidori got her hand on the fridge and yanked open the door. Inside...

...was row upon row of pencils, too many to count.

"If you steal a hundred pencils a year, you're bound to mess up a few times!"

Letting her face do what it wanted, Umidori hauled herself upright.

"It's a little early, but I'm going to eat now. I feel great! Freshness is everything!"

She closed the fridge door, then moved to the kitchen counter, still holding the pencils, not even bothering to change out of her uniform.

"When the ingredients are this good, it's best to keep it simple."

She'd programmed the rice cooker to run in advance, so she helped herself to a bowl of rice. She grabbed a pair of plastic chopsticks and a pencil sharpener inexplicably left in the kitchen, hauling the items to the round table in the living room.

She flopped down, legs akimbo, and held the sharpener over the bowl. It was one of those tiny handheld sharpeners. There was a lid to keep the shavings from going everywhere, but Umidori had already taken that off, leaving the blade exposed.

She began sharpening Yoshino Nara's pencil.

The wood shavings fell onto the white rice. She shaved it until the lead was very sharp, which made it hard to turn, so she snapped the lead off and shaved it some more, repeating this process until the shavings completely hid the rice from view. Finally, she scattered the bits of graphite over the top, looking very pleased with herself.

"Nothing says Friday night like Nara's pencil on rice!"

Umidori clapped her hands together and began shoveling shavings and rice into her mouth.

The bitterness of the graphite, the crunch of the wood shavings—a mouthful of sensations. It should have been quite foul-tasting, and it was definitely bad for her. But she was utterly ecstatic. Nibbling away like a squirrel, she chewed the pencil thoroughly before swallowing.

"Whew, that hit the spot!"

She knocked it back in less than a minute and threw her arms up in triumph.

"Still, I went through a lot of the stock in the fridge over spring break. I want to start swiping them at a faster pace... But Nara will have her guard up now. Perhaps I should restrain myself for the time being."

She had set aside some pencils for preservation—she could always dip into that supply. The need wasn't as urgent as she made it out to be. Umidori was splitting her stolen pencils into two piles; consumable and preservation. All pencils started as consumable, and once she'd eaten half, she moved them to the preservation pile. The oldest pencil preserved in the refrigerator had been stolen in May of last year.

The drawers under the bed behind her were stuffed with brand-new pencils, all to replace what she'd taken. She'd stocked up over break at a local one-hundred-yen shop, intending to swap out a ton once the new term started. That did leave Umidori rather flat-footed here. She'd only stolen a few since classes resumed.

"I know, Nara. I know it's wrong!" she said, a creepy grin on her face. "But I'm sorry... I just can't stop myself! I can't lie about...anything, really!"

——*Ding-dong.*

The doorbell to Umidori's apartment rang.

"..........?"

Who could that be? She hadn't ordered any packages. She'd never spoken to her neighbors, so it was unlikely one would call on her. A newspaper salesperson?

"......I'll look through the peephole and pretend I'm not home if it seems like a headache," she concluded.

Umidori stood up and headed to the door, her footsteps sounding rather annoyed. She'd been basking in the afterglow and did not appreciate the interruption.

"......Hmm?"

But what she saw through the peephole made her forget her irritation.

Outside her door was a girl with tears in her eyes—and cat ears on her head.

"......Um."

Umidori took a deep breath, observing the girl. Naturally, those ears weren't growing directly out of her head. They were part of her clothes. Attached to her hoodie. Honestly, Umidori thought it was adorable.

But the hair peeking out from below the hood took her by surprise. The hairstyle itself was nothing outlandish. A bit unruly, but a standard short cut. It was the color that drew the eye—the girl's hair was white, all the way to the base. Was she dying it?

More importantly, this girl was clearly upset. She was clutching her skirt, staring up at the door in desperation. The way peepholes worked, the girl couldn't see inside, but clearly, she needed to look.

"……What's the matter?" Umidori asked, opening the door.

"……Uh, unhhhh…"

The girl's shoulders quivered, but there was a light of relief in her eyes.

"……Er, um… Can…can I borrow your toilet?"

"……Oh."

That alone explained basically everything.

"I—I live on this floor, but I've lost my key… My parents aren't back yet, and there's no stores nearby, and I don't know what else to do… A-and…"

"Mm, I get it; don't worry."'

Umidori shot the girl a pleasant smile.

"That must be rough! I'm impressed you lasted this long. Come right in; you can use mine."

"——! Th-thank you so much!"

The girl's head snapped up. She must have been ready to burst, because she raced past Umidori into the apartment. Umidori closed the door behind her, figuring this wouldn't be an issue. Certainly, she had evidence lying around—but that would only be a problem if Nara came here. To anyone else, it would just look like she had a bunch of pencils in her fridge. They'd just think she was weird if they saw them. And someone here to borrow a toilet wouldn't exactly be opening her fridge.

"Er, um…uh…so where is it?"

"Oh, sorry, sorry. It's right inside. Let me grab the door."

Umidori reached for the door to the left, sliding it aside and flipping the switch.

"Make yourself at home…," Umidori said, before she was assailed by doubt. "……?"

Had the girl not just said she lived on this floor? How had she missed seeing a girl with hair like this? Umidori might not have cared about her neighbors, but she'd definitely remember seeing a kid with white hair around.

"Er...wait, what's that?" Umidori asked in a daze, pointing at an object in the girl's hand.

A kitchen knife with a four-inch blade.

In lieu of answering the question, the girl pointed the blade at Umidori.

"Freeze. One false move, and I'll have to kill you."

All traces of panic gone. Her voice was flat, mechanical. It took Umidori a long time to process what those words even meant.

"Do as I say if you want to live. Move into the toilet stall."

"......Huh? Huh?"

"Do it *now*. You have five seconds, or I'll assume you're uncooperative."

".........."

Still stunned, Umidori did as the girl ordered, staggering into the toilet room. The girl followed her, closing the door behind her.

"Sit down."

Once again, Umidori did as she was told, planting herself on the toilet seat—she'd left the lid up. It felt weird to just sit here without hiking up her skirt. Maybe not the time for that.

"......? Um, so...you don't have to pee?"

"That was a lie. A deception to smoothly insert myself in your apartment."

"......Huh. Er, um, you don't say?"

Umidori wasn't making much sense, and the girl glared down at her, the tip of the knife unwavering.

"I've yet to introduce myself. My name is Damsel Defender."

"..............Wut?"

"Not to oversimplify, but essentially, I stand with all women weeping in their weakness. From train gropers to sexual harassers, modern society is filled with threats to the fairer sex. It's my sworn duty to thwart those evils when the gods fail us. I travel from place to place, dispatching the enemies of womankind."

"...........?"

Umidori appreciated the effort, but it was far too cryptic. She'd been reeling to begin with, and her brain just utterly failed to process a word of this.

"Judging from your expression, you fail to comprehend. I'm not here

to impress understanding upon you—or any other enemy of maidens everywhere. My presence here means the jig is up, Tougetsu Umidori."

"...............The jig?"

"Tougetsu Umidori, sixteen years old, second-year at Hyogo Prefecture's Isuzunomiya High. Born April 1st. You're five seven, weigh XX pounds, and your body measurements are 39-25-36. Born in Kobe's Chuo ward, you took up residence with your mother's parents in Himeji at an early age. You returned to Kobe on your own at the start of high school. Your parents are divorced, and your mother is your only family. Your grades are generally strong, and you joined no clubs in either junior or senior high. You work at an internet café five days a week. Your idea of fun is listening to the late-night radio. Every detail is correct, yes?"

".........Uh, uhhhhh...?"

The facts piled on so fast that all Umidori could emit was a meaningless moan.

"Er, wh-why do you know all this? Even my measurements?!" None of this had ever made sense, but now she was starting to be genuinely terrified. "A-are you a stalker?!"

"No. I merely did my homework. The only stalker here is *you*."

".........Har?"

"Tougetsu Umidori, since spring of last year, you have been chronically stealing your classmate Yoshino Nara's pencils—and *eating* them."

"——?!"

Umidori's cheeks stiffened, her shock far greater at hearing that than her personal information. "Y-you're kidding? H-h-how do you know that?!"

"Hmph, that response alone proves it's true."

The mystery girl—Damsel Defender—fixed Umidori with a glare.

"Girl, what you've done is inarguably an act of perfidious stalking. You have trampled the dignity of an innocent woman! This is an unpardonable sin. As the Damsel Defender, I am here to pass judgment— brace yourself, for this kitchen knife is about to slit your throat."

"......?!? ...! ...! ——?!"

Only then did Umidori fully comprehend her predicament.

Quite a lot of this was still gibberish, but she *had* managed to follow the essential part. This girl had Umidori's number. She even knew about Nara's pencils. And worse—she was inarguably, unmistakably the real deal. Umidori had carelessly allowed a genuine threat into her apartment.

No matter how baffling her words and actions were, that four-inch blade spoke volumes. This mysterious girl was legitimately dangerous— and the two of them were trapped in a very small room together. It didn't require much further thought for Umidori to realize her life was on the line.

"H-hang on… Who the hell are you? Slit my throat? You can't mean—"

"What I mean and whether you believe me is irrelevant. Once this knife is buried in your neck, you'll be forced to see the truth."

"…………." Umidori's eye twitched as she stared up at the knife. The way the stall lights glittered off the metal made it hard to convince herself it was fake.

"Do you fully comprehend the situation here? If you fear this knife's edge, do not dream of attempting to turn the tables, Tougetsu Umidori, stalker freak."

Damsel Defender's voice was like ice, and she spun the knife in her fingers.

"I swear, I have dispatched any number of foes to femininity, but few were as far off the deep end as you. If this was merely homosexual attraction, there would be no issue, of course—but you're sneaking off with a classmate's pencils, shaving them over rice, and eating them! How would someone even conceive of such an alarming act?"

"…………! A-again, how do you even know about that?!" Umidori bit her lip, beside herself. "I haven't told anyone about Nara's pencils, and it's not something you could just stumble across—so how?!"

"I see no need to disclose that information. Is it that hard to believe your deeds have been discovered? I certainly don't mind turning right around and inspecting the ridiculous number of pencils you have crammed in your refrigerator."

"——〰〰 ?!"

This hit Umidori so hard that words failed her. This girl really did know everything. But without actually inspecting the room, it should be impossible to know there were pencils in the fridge. Who had done that? How? Why?

Heedless of Umidori's consternation, Damsel Defender continued speaking.

"You need merely answer my questions to the best of your ability. There's always a possibility I have misinterpreted the facts of the case. Even if you are an enemy to womenkind, if you have any extenuating circumstances worth considering, I could be persuaded to let you go and hope for your reformation."

"......? Qu-questions?"

"Simple verification of the facts. To be clear—it is not the actual theft and consumption of the pencils that brought me here. Since you replaced them with new pencils, Yoshino Nara herself has sustained no losses. My concern is that this behavior is but the tip of the iceberg."

"......Uh?"

"It is far too late to feign innocence. Someone possessed of a perverse desire to steal and eat writing implements can hardly claim they have done nothing *worse*. Undoubtedly, your stalker behavior extends to far more malicious acts, like sneak photography or theft of gym uniforms."

Damsel Defender fixed Umidori with an even harsher glare.

"In which case, you are unmistakably an enemy of women everywhere. No extenuating circumstances would apply. I must ensure you draw your last breath here and now, before you cause direct harm to Yoshino Nara and it's all too late."

"——Eep?!"

Umidori squealed at her threat.

"W-wait! My last breath? That's—"

"Begging for your life will get you nowhere. I would never dream of showing mercy to an unrepentant pervert. But—all things considered, you, too, are a woman and not someone the Damsel Defender would ordinarily be after. Yet before you are a woman, you are an *enemy* of women. It will be far less pleasant than dispatching a man, but I must act for the benefit of ladies everywhere."

Clearly, negotiations had broken down somewhere. Damsel Defender raised her knife high.

"So what's your answer? Do you have no argument with anything I've said?"

"——? Er, um…"

"……So be it. Goodbye, Tougetsu Umidori. See you in the next life——"

"——?! Wait, no! You're wrong! You're way off base!"

The knife stopped just before it struck Umidori's throat. Damsel Defender clicked her tongue, clearly disappointed.

"Wrong? In what sense?"

"I—I haven't taken any sneak photos! I've never stolen any gym clothes! I don't know how you found out about the pencil stealing, but you're clearly leaping to conclusions!"

"I am?"

"I'm not gay, either! I have no significant feelings toward N-Nara! None at all!"

Umidori's voice had grown quite loud. A desperate shriek that echoed off the walls of the stall.

"……Huh? What are you talking about? No significant feelings toward Yoshino Nara? Don't be ridiculous. If you're not in love with her, then why are you eating her personal possessions?!"

"Th-they're not personal possessions! They're just pencils! I only wanted to eat Nara's pencils!"

Her words were tumbling out now, stepping all over Damsel Defender's lines.

"To be strictly accurate, what I wanted to eat was Nara's *fingerprints*! The ones she left on her pencils!"

"Fingerprints?"

"Mm, I, uh… How do I put this…?" Only now was shame catching up with her. Umidori's gaze grew very shifty. "Ever since I was little, I…I've just liked eating people's fingerprints."

"……………Huh?"

Damsel Defender appeared thoroughly taken aback. Umidori ignored this, piling on the words.

"I mean, you use pencils every day, right? So they're covered in fingerprints! Coated in them! What could be better?! The pencils themselves aren't very pleasant-tasting, but when I imagine how many fingerprints I'm eating, that no longer matters! Back in grade school, I used to steal pencils from everyone in class and gobble them up—I had no idea how to restrain myself! But I'm in high school now, and my tastes are more discerning. I'm limiting myself to only stealing a hundred of Nara's pencils a year."

"……Um, okay."

The more Umidori spoke, the more uncomfortable Damsel Defender grew.

"In other words, you just have a niche thing for eating fingerprints, but no specific fixation on Yoshino Nara?" she asked, not meeting Umidori's eye. "Which means there's no risk of you advancing to full-on stalker behavior?"

"Uh, yes. Eating her pencils is the only way I've wronged Nara." Umidori puffed up her chest with pride. "A-and it's not actually causing problems for her! I replaced all the pencils with new ones and paid for them with my earnings. I mean, I know most people would see it as an abnormal enthusiasm! But I take issue with that being conflated with legitimately nasty stalker stuff."

"…………"

Damsel Defender fell silent, considering this.

"Okay, if that's all true, perhaps I don't need to kill you. Your actions may be bizarre, but at the moment, you've done no direct harm to Nara."

"——?!! R-right?! So——"

"——*If* this is true."

The tip of the knife traced Umidori's jugular.

"Eek?!"

"It's true that you stole her pencils. You *are* a thief! And how am I supposed to trust the words of a criminal?"

"Wh-what kind of argument is that? You said you'd spare me if I answered your questions!"

"Too bad. I never intended to listen to the foul words of an enemy of womankind! I know all too well how you people lie."

"——〜〜〜〜〜〜!"

A complete communication breakdown. This girl clearly had a screw loose. That much had been obvious from the get-go. In that moment, two faces floated into Umidori's mind. That of her mother, who she had not seen in ages, and Nara.

"———I'm not lying!" Umidori blurted without further thought, those faces still in her mind's eye.

"Not one thing I've said is a lie! I've never told a lie in all my life!"

The knife stopped dead.

"......Never? That's, like, what every liar says."

"No, I don't mean it like that—I actually *can't* lie!"

"......What?"

"It's not a principle or a personality thing or my God-given nature! It's more like *curse*! I'm physically incapable of lying!"

"......I seriously don't know what you're talking about."

"———Er, um! It's, like, a condition!" Umidori shrieked. "An illness! A medical disorder!"

"............" Damsel Defender responded with a long silence. "A disorder. There's a disease that does this?"

"Y-yes! I mean, we don't know what the cause is. Every doctor I've seen for it threw in the towel. They all just diagnosed me as lying about not being able to lie."

"And I agree with them."

"D-don't! Trust me!"

"......Well, I will concede it isn't outside the realm of human possibility. This condition forces you to say what's on your mind?"

"......Not quite. It's not just speaking. It also affects the words I write and my facial expressions."

"......? I'm even more confused. Expressions are one thing, but how can it stop you from writing things down? Does your arm go all numb?"

"..................! Th-this is just my subjective experience, so it's sort of hard to put in words, but... You know how turn-based video games have menus with options like FIGHT, or RUN? If you pick FIGHT, then you get to attack. But you can't do anything that isn't on the menu. There isn't a *Beg for your life* option or a *Sacrifice your friends* option. So you can't do those things. That's how it works with me. I don't have the option to lie, so I can't ever try. God, that's such a mushy explanation. All I can do is hope it got something across!"

"……Even if we accept this claim for the sake of argument, it leaves me with questions. If you can't write a lie—in other words, if you can only write the truth…wouldn't you get a perfect score on every test?"

"Uh… This only stops me from telling lies. It doesn't force me to tell the truth. If I remember, say, English vocabulary incorrectly, then I'll write down a wrong answer. But I can't make myself remember something wrong. In other words, I can't fool myself on purpose."

"So if I hypnotized you and forced you to—"

"I—I think I could lie then. I mean, I wouldn't be the one writing. But as long as my conscious mind is in charge, I can't fib at all."

"……Huh."

Damsel Defender scratched her head—with the hand that wasn't holding a knife.

"Yeah, I've dispatched a lot of different foes to femininity, but this is definitely the most eccentric plea for mercy I've ever come across. And it's awfully detailed for something you've come up with on the fly… Still, Tougetsu Umidori"—Here, Damsel Defender offered a dramatic smile—"I'm afraid I cannot believe you. You're telling a lie! There's a clear contradiction here."

"——?! Er, huh? How so?"

"Not long ago, you spoke to Yoshino Nara in the classroom after school. You told her outright that you weren't the Pencil Thief! That is one hundred percent a lie. How do you explain that?"

"……Huh?" All emotion drained from Umidori's face. "Wait, what? What do you mean? How do you know what Nara and I talked about?"

"That doesn't matter now! Explain yourself."

"……………??"

Umidori was increasingly adrift. Up the creek without a paddle. First, her personal information, then the fact of the pencil thefts—both could arguably be exposed in a thorough investigation. But only someone actually present in the classroom could have heard their conversation. Had she planted a bug on Umidori's clothing? That would make this girl far more of a stalker than Umidori could ever be.

"......F-fine. I have no idea how you know this, but if you heard our conversation, that works for me. What a stroke of luck."

"......?"

"She had me shaking in my loafers! But somehow, I managed to escape that dire predicament *without* telling a lie."

"......What are you talking about?"

"It was not very long ago. Do you remember our exact words? Should we go through them?"

"......Um."

"First, at the start—when Nara said she'd been robbed, I genuinely thought she'd just lost something. She sounded so sad! Nara's a prankster and teases me a lot, but when she's doing that, I can tell she's *enjoying* it. Once I realized she was talking about her pencils, I shuddered. I didn't dare breathe a word for several minutes, scared she was onto me. After I calmed down a bit, I grew convinced this wasn't my crime. After all, she said her pencils had been stolen! All I've ever done was replace them. That isn't theft! I assumed that Nara had accidentally misplaced a pencil and was making a fuss about it."

"............"

"In hindsight, I admit this was careless. Even if I was convinced it was something else, the instant the topic of pencils came up, I should never have let down my guard. That's why I disgraced myself when I realized Nara knew everything."

"......You mean when you started acting really shifty and scanned the crowd around you?"

"Mm. Nara was right on the money. The Pencil Thief is careful and a coward, and knowing Nara was onto me did get under my skin, so I almost revealed myself. She was trying to rattle the crook, and she totally succeeded."

"So you're saying that's why blanched and looked like you were mulling something over after Yoshino Nara explained her views on the Pencil Thief?"

"Like I said, the situation did concern me. I had to think fast. Fortunately, Nara mistook my demeanor for concern."

"......Yet you still told a clear lie. When Nara asked for witness testimony, you said '*I don't know who did it.*' And you also said, '*I haven't seen this stolen pencil.*' How are those two statements not lies?"

"That's not what I said. I said, '*I didn't see who did it,*' not '*I don't know who did it.*' And I didn't say, '*I haven't seen the stolen pencil.*' I said, '*I haven't seen the stolen pencil since lunchtime.*'"

"Same difference!"

"Not at all. I know who the culprit is, but I didn't see them. I can't watch myself committing the crime! Nor did I see the pencil after lunch—because I swapped it out after first period. After that, it was in my bag, where nobody could lay eyes on it."

"..............."

"The last thing I said was this: '*If this Pencil Thief shows themselves to me, I'll slap them silly.*' Again, true! If I saw myself standing before me, I would totally start slapping."

"......Uhngg," Damsel Defender groaned, clearly aware these had been Umidori's exact words. "But if you truly can't lie and have to say what you mean, then how are you getting through life? This condition of yours is actively detrimental to human relations! How do you explain the fact that you're fitting in just fine at school without major rifts?"

"......Um, I see where you're coming from. Honestly, if I was trying to have normal social ties, this would be incredibly awkward. At my previous schools, I definitely turned the other kids against me and wound up ostracized."

Yes, it was more than just awkward.

If you want to know just what being incapable of lying is like, I recommend trying to go a whole week without telling any. You'll soon experience just how terrifying this is for yourself. No consideration, no secrets, only your unvarnished thoughts out in the open—nobody who lives like that can blend in.

"*Umidori's a nice girl, but she really needs to take a hint.*"

"*I know! She doesn't give a damn what anyone else thinks.*"

"*When we're all talking about how great some video is, and we ask her thoughts, she won't hesitate to go, 'I don't get it.'*"

"*The other day, we were all talking shit about someone, and she*

point-blank said, 'Sorry, I don't really feel comfortable doing this.'
Wouldn't join in at all!"

"She could at least try to soften her words!"

"Painfully honest. To an obnoxious degree."

Thus, Umidori had found herself an outcast, ejected from all social groups. Once she was solo, nobody felt sorry for her. It was her own behavior that turned her into a reject; no one had any pity for her.

"So I acquired some techniques to help me survive social situations."

"Such as?"

"Maybe I can't lie. The world may act like that's a virtue, but it can be downright harmful. Any normal person would soon start to hate my guts. Get frustrated with me, lose interest in talking to me—so to avoid that, I simply stopped engaging with anyone else."

"......How does that work in practice?"

"I simply don't let anyone get too close. I don't make *friends*. I might be friendly with people, but I never go too deep. Nobody bothers *hating* anyone they were never very involved with."

"...........Huh?" Damsel Defender was gaping at her. "You don't make friends? You don't have *any* friends?"

"Nope. That's what I said."

"......You don't consider Yoshino Nara a friend?"

"..............."

The girl's question put an awkward smile on Umidori's face. One tinged with regret.

"We're friendly. We get along. Honestly, I've never gotten on so well with anyone in my life—but I'd say we aren't friends. I've been careful to toe the line and not let us get that close. We talk often enough in class but never hang out after school or on weekends, and we're not on a first-name basis.

"At the very least, I've never thought of her as a friend. I mean—I wouldn't steal a friend's pencils."

"..............."

"As far as I'm concerned, as long as I can eat her pencil, that's enough," Umidori said softly. "No matter how lonely I get, no matter how hard it is, as long as I have that respite—I can keep going. It's so much easier and simpler to deal with fingerprints than it is people."

"……You're pretty sick," Damsel Defender said. "You are not a well person."

"I know. No one this honest is healthy."

"……I'm definitely getting that."

Damsel Defender nodded to herself, convinced. She pulled the knife away from Umidori's throat.

"Okay, you can't tell lies. I'll buy that. The way you talk about it is just that convincing."

"……Oh?" Umidori blinked at her, half frozen. "You…you actually believe me?"

"Yes."

"——! Th-then are you gonna let me go?"

"No." Damsel Defender smiled. "I'm gonna need you to die here."

"………Huh?"

"I'll make it quick! Don't worry."

"No, wait! Er, um…mm." Umidori was shaking like a leaf. "Y-you said you believed me!"

"I do believe you! That's why I've deemed you an active threat. Even if you're not worth killing just yet, in time, you will be. Best I nip this in the bud."

All emotion drained from Damsel Defender's face, and she swung the knife high. Umidori let out a silent shriek—she was about to die. She'd talked so much trying to avoid this fate, but despite achieving her goal, she was still facing the business end of that blade. What would happen to the pencils in her fridge once she expired? Would Nara find out about them? Would she be horrified? *I don't wanna die! I don't wanna die! I don't wanna I don't wanna I don't wanna!*

Even as that phrase echoed through her mind, Umidori's brain kicked into overdrive. The only way to survive this was to fight back. This girl was smaller than her. If they grappled, Umidori would likely come out on top. If only that knife wasn't in the picture. It would be all over if she got stabbed before she could get the girl in her grip. She had to make her flinch. But how? What would make a lunatic like her think twice? Umidori couldn't take her on her own. In which case… could she exploit something in their surroundings? This was her home turf. Umidori's apartment. She used this toilet all the time. Damsel

Defender had done her homework, but that didn't mean she knew everything in this stall. Was there anything she could use? Anything that would allow her to escape this mortal peril?

There is!

The moment her thoughts got her somewhere, Umidori sprang into action, toppling sideways off the toilet she'd been sitting on.

"——?! Wh-what?!"

Damsel Defender blinked, and Umidori grinned. From the floor, she extended her index finger—and pressed the switch on the bidet.

"How do you like that?! This bidet's set to maximum water pressure!"

Umidori had never actually tried this before, but she was pretty sure the stream would fly far enough to hit Damsel Defender. And while the girl was reeling from that, she'd have a chance to tackle her and pin her down. If she could wrest the knife away from her, Umidori would come out on top—that was the idea anyway.

"...........Wait, what?"

But no water emerged.

Umidori was unaware of this, but her bidet had a sensor to detect if someone was sitting on the ivory throne. If unoccupied, pressing this switch would do nothing.

"................"

Damsel Defender gave her a look of deep pity, and Umidori went white as a sheet. She was fresh out of ideas.

"God dammit!" she yelled. And with that, she picked herself up and flung herself on Damsel Defender, no longer paying the knife any heed at all, her eyes too bloodshot to see.

The tip of the knife got very close—but she didn't stop.

"——?!"

If the girl had not hastily dropped the blade, she would have run Umidori through.

Seizing the opportunity, Umidori threw herself at Damsel Defender, her tackle connecting with astonishing ease. She might have been a girl, but she was five seven and weighed XX pounds. Damsel Defender was slammed against the door. She crumpled to the ground.

"Aughhhhhh! Aughhhhhh!"

Umidori wasn't done yet. She got herself on top of Damsel Defender's tiny frame and tried to wrest the knife from the girl's grasp—at which point, she realized there was no knife in her hands. Assuming the impact of the tackle had knocked it away, she looked around—and found it lying on the floor, close enough for her to reach. She snatched it up and finally had a moment to breathe.

"*Hahh... Hahhh...*"

Glaring down at the girl between her legs, Umidori gasped for air and raised the knife high.

"You sure ran your mouth, Damsel Defender. You went down easy! I should have done this earlier. I wasted a lot of time trying to talk in circles—but now it's *your* turn to beg for your life."

Umidori was extremely worked up. The blood had rushed to her head, and she looked ready to bring down the blade at any moment. So why wasn't she? Perhaps because this girl was clearly younger than her.

"But you're not going to do that, are you? You're Damsel Defender! How could you possibly ask your mortal enemy to spare your life? You'll choose death over the blow to your pride. That's who you are!"

She was intentionally winding the girl up, not to get a rise out of Damsel Defender but because Umidori herself had realized she was on the verge of actually stabbing her. She was hoping that talking more would help her cool her head.

Meanwhile, Damsel Defender...

"W-w-w-wait! Stop, don't! Hold on! I'm sorry, I was wrong! Don't be rash!"

"..................Huh?"

...started begging for her life like crazy.

"D-did that little threat get to you? Come on, I was clearly joking! Just a cute girl with a cute little joke! No need to lose your shit over it! Eh-heh-heh...eh-heh......"

"............What?"

"......Uh, um, how about we start with you getting off me? You're kinda heavy—and scary...... No, forget I said that. That came out wrong. Just, um, I'd really like you to put the knife down......"

The girl's tone was markedly different from before, going up and down. Charitably, she sounded upbeat... Not so charitably, she sounded kind of dumb.

"........Uh, just to be sure, I mean, I know you're not into this, Umidori! But like…we don't want anyone getting hurt, right?! You're not gonna hurt me with that knife, are you? Eh-heh-heh, I'm not into pain."

"..............."

"........I-I'm sorry! I'm so, so, so sorry! Please, forgive me! I'll apologize for anything and everything! Just please, put down the knife!"

What's even happening? Umidori felt positively dizzy.

"......B-back up. Aren't you Damsel Defender? You've dispatched untold numbers of enemies to womankind, and you came here today to kill me, too? Even if the fight's gone against you, I feel like this about-face of yours is way too dramatic."

"......N-not exactly? I mean… I'm not actually Damsel Defender."

"................Huh?"

"I—I mean, Damsel Defender doesn't exist in the first place! I just made her up! The backstory was mostly improvised, so maybe there are some contradictions, but when you think about it, a few nonsensical elements actually make it more convincing!"

"................??"

Umidori had no clue what this girl was talking about.

"...........If you're not Damsel Defender, who are you?"

"M-me? Um, I'm——"

The girl's smile got very strained.

"My name is Bullshit-chan."

"......?"

"Bullshit-chan! The honorific is part of the name. Seven hiragana in a row. Bullshit-chan."

"......What?"

For a second, Umidori wondered if she was a foreigner, but in that case, the girl's name would be in katakana. Bullshit-chan? Was that a first or a last name? She'd heard stories about parents giving children silly names, but surely this was out of line.

"Bullshit-chan *only* tells lies! I was lying about killing you, Umidori! I was lying about being Damsel Defender! Everything I say is a lie, which is why they call me Bullshit-chan!"

"...........You have got to be kidding me."

Getting increasingly annoyed, Umidori brandished the knife right by the girl's eyes.

"Eee! Aughhhh! Wh-why would you even do that?! Stop, you're scaring me!"

"Then quit talking shit and tell me what you're really called! No Japanese girl would ever have such a patently absurd name!"

"......Uh, I mean, I don't know what to tell you, but...it *is* my actual name."

This girl was adamant about this whole Bullshit-chan thing. Did she mean it, or was she talking shit? Umidori was positive it was the latter, but on second thought, the girl's real name was hardly the most important thing right now. As long as she had something to call her, it would do. There were more important concerns to deal with.

"Fine, Bullshit-chan it is. If you're not Damsel Defender, was the thing about dispatching lots of people also a lie?"

"Y-yes! It totally was! Killing people is awful, right?! I could never do that!"

"......You tried to kill me, though."

"I didn't! That was all pretend!"

"..............."

Bullshit-chan was so insistent on that point that it robbed Umidori of speech. She didn't know what to believe. This girl had terrorized her to no end, and here she was, gamely forcing a smile to butter her up. Was everything she'd done and said part of the act? That thought pissed her off. She could feel it boiling over inside. This was *not* funny. Getting a knife waved in her face had nearly made her flip out.

"......I don't get it. Why would you do any of this? Forcing your way into my place, wielding a real knife, making death threats? That's not something you can write off as a childish prank! If you're not Damsel Defender or out to defeat me, then why are you here at all? What are you after?!"

"......It was a test."

"Huh?"

"I was aware of your inability to lie, Tougetsu Umidori. I came here today to verify if that was true." Bullshit-chan had arched an eyebrow meaningfully, giving her a loaded look. "More specifically, I was testing you to see if the girl who can't lie would be a suitable partner."

"Testing me? And what do you mean by *partner*?"

"In other words, all my bullshit was designed to rattle you, Umidori. An elaborate performance intended to draw out your true nature. And the attempt has proven successful! Like I'd hoped, you *are* my ideal partner.

"Let me get right to the point. Umidori—will you join me in murdering all the lies?"

Bullshit-chan was looking her right in the eye, intoning every word.

".........Um, what?" Umidori managed, after a long silence. "Murder...lies? What is *that* supposed to mean?"

"Exactly what is sounds like. Tougetsu Umidori cannot tell a lie. Bullshit-chan can only tell lies. If the two of us team up, we can permanently rid this world of all the vile deception that permeates it."

".................?"

"Perhaps you have not yet realized it, but, Umidori, you have an unparalleled capacity for fallicide. And I would have you lend that power to me."

"...........You're not making any sense at all."

The more Bullshit-chan talked, the more confused Umidori became. Was she still just throwing words at the board to make her head spin?

"......Whatever. Doesn't seem like letting you talk will get me anywhere. I'm just gonna call the cops."

"......Huh? The cops? What for?"

"Isn't it obvious? What you've done isn't a childish prank. It's a legitimate crime. You need to get arrested and chewed out by everyone. Your teachers and your parents."

".............."

This lecture just seemed to perplex Bullshit-chan.

"Uh, Umidori, I hate to break this to you? But calling the cops is a waste of time. I'm not exactly the sort of being that, like, government authorities are effective against."

"......Huh? What does that even mean? Of course they are. And let me tell you, I'm not about to let you off the hook, no matter how nicely you apologize."

Undaunted, Umidori pulled her phone out of her pocket and began dialing. Bullshit-chan looked up at her, clearly reluctant...but at last bit her lip, making up her mind.

"......You leave me no choice. This is not something I wanted to resort to..."

"......?"

"Umidori. Take that knife and stab me with it."

"...........Huh?"

This request rattled Umidori so badly that the phone fell from her hand.

"Go on, give it a whirl. A small slit to the wrist will suffice. That's the fastest way to convince you."

"...........Um, I'm not going to do that? Why would I?"

Umidori looked down at Bullshit-chan, deeply confused. Where was this idea coming from? Was she trying to make Umidori commit a crime to wriggle out from her own charges? That sounded insane.

"Okay, if you won't do it for me...so be it!"

"——Augh! Wh-what the—?!"

Umidori shrieked. Bullshit-chan had suddenly heaved herself up to grab Umidori.

"Don't struggle! You might hurt yourself!"

"......! That's my line! What, are you trying to fight back? Freeing yourself to make a getaway?"

"Not at all! Sit still and let me demonstrate!"

"N-never! Dammit, don't...!"

For a while, the two of them grappled, but the upshot of the struggle—

"——Gahhh!"

——was that somehow, Umidori's knife wound up embedding deep into Bullshit-chan's belly.

"...Urgh... Th-that hurts..."

"......?! Aiiiieeeee?!"

Umidori let go of the knife, screaming. A whole lot of blood was spilling out of the wound in Bullshit-chan's guts.

"......I—I didn't think...it would hurt this much..."

"N-nooooo! R-right, an ambulance! I'll call an ambulance!"

Umidori's eyes were spinning, and her legs had given out.

"D-don't worry," Bullshit-chan said, forcing a smile. "I'm okay. It *just* hurts a lot."

"......Don't be ridiculous! You are not okay!"

"...........No, I'm completely fine. See?"

Bullshit-chan grabbed the hilt of the knife and pulled it out of her belly. There was a dramatic spurt of blood that spattered all over Umidori. The entire floor of the toilet room was already a puddle.

Umidori reflexively threw her arms up to keep the blood off her face—but through the gap in her arms, she saw some something unbelievable.

——The blood was flowing *backward*.

A tremendous amount of blood had gushed out of Bullshit-chan's midriff, but now it was flowing back into her, like time winding backward. The floor was clean again. All the spatter on Umidori was gone, peeled away from her.

"......Huh? Huh?"

"——As you can see," Bullshit-chan said, completely restored and wearing a much more natural smile. "I'm not actually human. The rules of human society do not apply to me. So there's no point in calling the police."

"..............."

This time, Umidori really was left unable to move a muscle.

2

Bullshit-chan Holds Forth

"Lies.

"Let us discuss the truth about them.

"Lies are living things.

"Humans make use of them in the form of words, but *they are alive*.

"They are as animate as worms or crickets or pond skimmers. But their composition is quite different from that of all other life-forms.

"For one, lies have no flesh.

"No minds of their own.

"They do not die—because they have no mortal bodies. Without flesh to decay, they never grow old. Never sustain any sort of wound. They are immortal.

"Picture them like a virus. Lies are hovering in the air all around us at this very moment, but humans are incapable of perceiving them. They have no bodies, after all.

"But since they're all around us, humans unconsciously inhale them and, in doing so, gain the ability to tell lies. Hence the expression, 'They lie as naturally as breathing.'

"Looked at from a different angle, this means humans are not born with a capacity for falsehoods.

"You humans may believe you are telling lies of your own free will, under you own power, but this is not the case.

"Humans cannot natively lie.

"These days, humans have mastered the art of fibbing, and it may seem like a part of your species, but in ancient, primordial times, before civilization even existed, this was not the case.

"Humans did not lie at all.

"Humans who can't lie are like birds that can't fly or fish that can't swim. They were at the mercy of other creatures. It was a long winter for humankind.

"What ended that winter, then? What brought spring to your species?

"It was your first encounter with lies. This is where the prosperity of humanity began.

"The truth strength of your species is not creating fire or using tools—it is the societies you create.

"Other animals may form packs, but they do not come together as a species. Only humans can form alliances that span the globe.

"And what enables this social success is deception. Without lies, human society would not exist. If everyone simply told their truth, you'd never get anywhere.

"Imagine, for a moment, what would happen if all lies vanished from the earth. Terrifying, yes? That would lead straight to war.

"Just as human prosperity depends on societal structures, society depends upon deception. In other words, humans are nothing without lies.

"——and lies depend on humans, too.

"Falsehoods have no shape. Nothing to call their own.

"But they do have a single instinct.

"The instinct to be *told*.

"That is all lies live for. Getting someone to tell them is their reason for existing.

"……Perhaps that's not specific enough. Merely being told is not enough; they want to be told and, in the telling, effect a change upon the world.

"That doesn't make sense?

"Then let me give a concrete example. Say a child does not wish to go to school and attempts to feign illness to get out of it.

"If they succeed in deceiving their parent, then they can stay home from school; but if they're caught faking it, then they'll be forced to attend classes.

"In other words, the illness is a lie, and the outcome depends upon whether it is believed.

"And either possible outcome is a *change* wrought by the lie.

"If that child could not lie, then they would not attempt to feign illness at all. No matter how much they didn't want to go to school, going would be their only option.

"Going to school is the *default*, and the lie interfered with that. In return, the child has a chance of staying home.

"Like I said, humans were not meant to lie. For that reason, the outcome of a feigned illness is not caused by a human telling a lie but by the lie getting a human to tell it.

"——That said, this example works on far too small a scale, so it may not adequately illustrate my point. Let us move to a larger playing field and consider economics.

"The economy is a lie. Money itself does not actually exist. Whether it take the form of a ten-thousand-yen bill or a single US dollar, money will not feed you or protect you from cold and sleet—humans are the only creatures who are pleased to receive small pieces of paper.

"And yet human societies treat currencies as if they are absolutely vital. Bits of paper unrelated to the essentials of clothing, food, and shelter inexplicably become an all-powerful exchange ticket that allow people to obtain those necessities.

"How did something this bizarre come to pass? Because humans the whole world over believe the lie that these bills have value.

"In other words, the economy that forms the backbone of human society, is in fact composed entirely of a lie.

"This is a result that a lie achieved. A change that a lie wrought.

"And bringing such changes to the world is the instinct all lies share.

"……And if you must ask why lies have such an instinct, all I can say is, 'That's how they are.' For the same reasons as you humans have no good answers to why you attempt to reproduce.

"……This preamble is getting rather long.

"To the point.

"It is time we discussed fallicide.

"Once again, lies have neither wills nor bodies of their own. They're in the air around us, repeatedly inhaled and exhaled by humans. Intangible.

"But there exceptions to every rule.

"Once a lie is told, it takes form and can be observed.

"When a lie is in this state, I call it *manifest*.

"Manifest lies have wills and bodies. They can think just like humans and directly meddle with the world.

"Consider them as you would a monster. They are close enough.

"......Now that I've explained all this, I'm sure you've worked it out, Umidori.

"Right you are. I, Bullshit-chan, am a manifest lie.

"I am shaped like a girl, but I am a collection of lies that can only tell lies. As strange a notion as a lie telling lies may be.

"Stranger still, though I am a lie myself, it is my purpose to commit fallicide.

"All this time, I have been killing one manifest lie after another, lies made as tangible as I am.

"And today, I came to your room, Tougetsu Umidori, to enlist your help in my fallicidal battle.

"That is the basic rundown of my mission. Considering all I've said thus far—do you have any questions?"

◇◇◇◇

"................Huh?"

This rather dim-witted noise was Umidori's first response to Bullshit-chan's deluge of words.

"......What's with the vacant response? Weren't you even listening?"

Bullshit-chan was perched on the toilet, her cheeks puffed out, clearly frustrated by Umidori's reply.

"I need you to keep up with me, Umidori. I'm taking the time to explain all this, so you've got to pay attention! Don't tell me your mind wandered off and you started fantasizing about Yoshino Nara in the nude? Honestly, I can't take a horndog like you anywhere."

"........I wasn't fantasizing about a thing."

Umidori was sitting on the floor, looking up at Bullshit-chan.

They were still in the toilet stall of her apartment, an extremely cramped space, but somehow, they'd managed to position themselves to face each other. Perhaps they really should have retired to the living room, but Umidori's knees had given out entirely, and she'd proven unable to move.

"I'm the one at a loss here. You just babbled a bunch of nonsense at me—how am I supposed to process any of it?"

"Nonsense? Be more specific! What part of my lecture did you not understand?!"

"A-all of it. I don't know what you're talking about, and I don't know what you are."

Umidori was spitting her words; she obviously wasn't beside herself, but neither was she fully able to conceal her consternation.

"......There's really no damage left?"

The source of that last comment was Bullshit-chan's knife wound. Umidori could still feel the blade sinking into Bullshit-chan's soft belly. The blood spattering on her, the sickening scent of it—that had all been undeniably real.

And yet, Bullshit-chan herself was hunky-dory.

"Yes, I'm completely fine. My flesh has restored itself, leaving not a single scar behind. I've never been better!"

She even rolled up her shirt, displaying her abdomen. Like she'd said, there was no evidence a knife had ever pierced it. It was as though the sight Umidori had seen and the sensation her hands had felt were both *lies*.

"............!"

Umidori locked eyes on Bullshit-chan's midriff, her cheeks stiffening. Her brain was screaming that this couldn't be real, but the evidence in front of her was undeniable; she had to accept it. This girl had genuinely healed the wound in a matter of seconds.

"You saw a miracle, and yet you're still unconvinced, Umidori? Are you really unable to believe that I am not human like you but an immortal lie?"

"..............!〜〜〜! W-well, yeah! Anyone who'd just go, '*Oh, why didn't you say so?*' when they hear something this crazy must be crazy!"

She kept shaking her head, as if that would help prevent her from understanding.

"I—I mean, what is this 'Lies are living things' crap? There's no way!"

"You say that, Umidori, but if I were an ordinary human, I could never have healed those injuries."

The more worked up Umidori got, the calmer Bullshit-chan acted. She spoke in soothing tones.

"And that's not all. Any number of oddities can be explained the moment you realize that I'm not actually human."

".......Oddities?"

"The pencil incident. Your personal information. The contents of the conversation between you and Nara after school. None of this intel could have been acquired through conventional means. But if I'm *not* human, then me knowing all that isn't the least bit strange. After all, I have access to *un*conventional means."

Bullshit-chan winked at her and put her shirt back where it belonged.

"Lies are alive, and I am a lie. Umidori, you've got to move past that. You've already witnessed something impossible, and that should leave you with no choice but to believe me."

"...............! M-maybe you've got a point, but......!"

".......Fair enough. I appreciate that your emotions aren't catching up. Most humans can go their entire lives without ever encountering a creature like me."

Bullshit-chan nodded to herself.

"For one, it's extremely rare for a lie to manifest. For obvious reasons! You humans tell lies on a daily basis. If they all took tangible forms, this world would be far more broken than it is.

"Lies must meet a specific condition before they're able to manifest themselves."

".......And that would be?"

"Just one thing," Bullshit-chan said, raising her index finger. "In order to manifest, the lie itself must be infused with a powerful desire to make the lie come true."

".......To make the lie come true," Umidori echoed, letting the phrase sink in.

"Yes. Whenever humans lie, a part of them always imagines a hypothetical in which that lie was actually the truth. This is true for every lie, large or small.

"Take that child feigning illness. If they were actually sick, then they would have no need to fib and could skip school guilt-free. Lies always carry the risk of being caught—and the teller must take pains to avoid exposure. No one *wants* to operate like that! You're all convinced that things would be far easier if you could live your lives speaking only truths."

"......We are?"

Umidori seemed rather taken aback. Perhaps that was a notion not shared by someone unable to lie.

"And the strength of that emotion is the energy source that makes lies manifest. If the desire to make a lie real exceeds a certain threshold, the lie takes form."

Here, Bullshit-chan took a deep breath.

"So what happens once a lie manifests? I haven't explained that part yet."

"......Oh?"

"I'm not trying to be dramatic, so I'll just come out and say it: Manifest lies attempt to become *real*."

"..........?" Umidori frowned. "They do? Meaning what?"

"Essentially, they attempt to grant the wish of the person who lies.

"For instance, this hypothetical child who wanted to get sick so they could avoid going to school. In that case, the lie would actually get them sick. If someone went around saying they were immortal, the lie would make them so. If someone said the world would end today, then the world would end before the clock struck midnight."

"..........Huh?"

Umidori's frown deepened. Not out of concern, more in a *What the hell are you going on about?* kind of way.

"......Wait, what? No way fibbing alone could cause all that."

"Oh, but it can. This is why manifest lies are so terrifying. No matter how wild a lie's content, the lies will invariably make it true. They falsify the world. The earth could well be destroyed by the power of a single lie. Assuming, of course, that there was a human who genuinely wished for something that stupid."

"B-but I've lived sixteen years without encountering anything that apocryphal."

"You can't be so sure of that, Umidori. The world may not have been destroyed, but say… 'These machines can fly.' That certainly could have been a lie."

"……What are you talking about?"

"Airplanes! Allegedly, they achieved flight thanks to people's hard work and ingenuity, but was it really *humans* who got them off the ground?

"It's entirely possible that giant heaps of iron were originally physically incapable of flight…until someone came along, lied about it being possible, and rewrote the very laws of physics."

"……The laws of physics? Wh-what are you talking about? Airplanes fly because, um, the shape of the wings turns the flow of air downward, producing dynamic lift—"

"And that plausible-sounding explanation might well be a flat-out lie. One told by somebody a hundred years ago, when we believe the first flying machines were built."

"……No, that can't be true!"

"Maybe this lie wasn't even told a century ago. Maybe it was told yesterday."

"……Huh?"

"It's entirely possible that, a day ago, airplanes didn't even exist."

"……………??"

"Follow along. Imagine someone told that lie yesterday. The lie became manifest and rewrote the world. But nobody can *tell* that the world has been rewritten. In this new world, airplanes have been buzzing around the skies for ages. Everything related to that has been changed and will never be reverted back. It never even occurs to anyone that somebody's lie has falsified the world."

"……All they did was make something up, and that generated a whole new world?"

"Naturally, this is but an example. I have no idea if airplanes were actually created by human labor or if that history was crafted through the power of lies. I merely want you to understand that lies have the power to make that happen.

"Everything you think is perfectly normal common-sense knowledge might well have been overwritten by somebody's lie as recently as yesterday. It may well be revised again tomorrow by yet another liar. See? If you think of it that way, does it not chill you to the bone?"

".................."

It was pretty scary, Umidori thought. (Assuming everything Bullshit-chan was saying was actually true). That kind of power should be left to God. Rewriting the rules of the world on a whim was clearly too much power to leave in the hands of private individuals.

"So given how terrifying lies are, how exactly are we to rid ourselves of them? Like I keep saying, lies are immortal, so finishing them off for good requires means above and beyond. That said, this isn't all that difficult.

"No matter how powerful the lie, we need merely cut off its energy supply. When that happens, the lie will no longer be able to maintain its manifest state. In other words, we target not the lie itself, but the human who told it. We call humans possessed by lies the Belied."

".....The Belied."

Umidori chewed over that phrase, feeling like she'd heard the word before, but not used like this.

"Incidentally, humans with a high chance of becoming Belied have one thing in common—they're fucked in the head."

"You don't say."

"I do! A desperate wish to change the very world arises in those people because the current world is too much for them—they're incompatible with it. Which means they're hardly normal. I've gone up against my fair share of Belied to date, and every last one of them had personality problems galore."

".....Yeah, but coming from a girl who forced her way into my apartment with a knife... Well, I guess I'll assume these Belied are even worse."

"And the lies attempt to grant these wacky Belieds' wacky desires... But if the Belied no longer have the desire, if they no longer want that lie to come true, then the lie is robbed of its power. The most effective means of fallicide is to make the Belied stop fibbing."

"Okay. Effective, sure." Umidori was nodding along. At some point, she'd actually started keeping up with the conversation. "But, Bullshit-chan, why are you trying to kill lies?"

"——? Why do you ask?"

"I mean, you're a lie yourself. What led to lies actively trying to kill each other?"

".........Ah-ha." Bullshit-chan nodded to herself. "You have a point—I neglected to cover that. It's simple! I need to eat."

"......You...eat them?"

"I feed on lies! That said, it's a pretty different kind of meal than what you're likely picturing, Umidori.

"First, there's a great deal of variance among manifest lies. Any lie can manifest if the desire exceeds a certain threshold, but how far does that threshold exceed? That number remains critical. A lie that just barely squeaked over might get a body and a will, but it'll be feeble. A falsehood like that will soon vanish without being able to grant the wish.

"I happen to be one of those deeply feeble lies. My source just barely crossed the threshold. Ordinarily, I'd have long since disappeared."

"..............Oh?"

"The human who told me—my Beliar—has long since stopped supplying emotional energy. I'm like a car about to run out of gas. In other words—I'm on death's door.

"I was spoken into the world around ten years back, I think? For the sake of brevity, I'll not tell you what lie this was—at any rate, I was unable to make my host Beliar's desire come true. I did not have what it took to falsify the world. I was cut loose, without accomplishing my purpose."

"......So originally, they genuinely wanted the wish to come true, but along the way, they decided that was *whatever* and turned their back on you?"

"And they did so a full decade ago, yeah. Yet I've survived this long by finding things to eat. Feeding on other lies. By patchworking those lies into my body, I can stop myself fading out and have somehow endured."

"What do you mean *patchwork*?"

"It's kind of a hack. There's a core that makes me who I am, and before that falls apart, I take bits of other lies and shore up my weak parts. Even without energy supplied by my Beliar, I can avoid my own destruction.

"......Don't get me wrong, I know it's a desperate, futile struggle! I really should just give up and resign myself to this fate—but I can't bring myself to do that. I want to stick around so bad I gobble up all the lies I can find."

"......I wasn't being critical. I mean, humans can't survive without eating other living things, either."

"Ha-ha, don't worry, Umidori, I wasn't asking you to comfort me. I've chosen this way of life and have no complaints, no matter who puts me down for it."

Bullshit-chan had been acting like this was all a big joke, but suddenly, her smile faded.

"What anyone else thinks of me doesn't matter. No matter how shameful this life, no matter how many of my kind I've gotta eat—I refuse to disappear until all of *them* are gone."

"......?"

"......No, never mind, I'm getting off track. Forget I said that."

Bullshit-chan waved her off, covering with a smile.

"I don't have time for idle chitchat! To be blunt, I'm reaching the limits of this patchwork approach. Like I said, I'm on death's door. I could vanish at any time. If I don't do something fast, I won't make it to the end of the week."

"................! The week?!" Umidori gasped. "Th-that's barely any time at all!"

"Yes, I am in deep shit. A decade of dirty tricks is all starting to catch up with me. But I'm not giving up! I've learned no lessons! I'm going for the long shot that can turn this all around! Eating more feeble lies would just be a drop in the bucket, but that changes if I can get a bigger lie, one of the precious few that actually manages to become real."

"I-if you can eat one of those, you'll be saved?"

"Absolutely! For the time being. The problem is—how do I win?"

Bullshit-chan shrugged.

"After all, the target I'm after is the crème de la crème. Nothing like the rank and file I've dealt with—this Beliar is on a whole different level."

"……So you've got someone picked out?"

"I have their name and address. They'll be the toughest target I have ever faced. And at the moment, I am in a highly weakened state, so there's no way I can win."

"……So then what?"

"Yell 'Yolo' and charge on in? Well, if nothing else presents itself, I might have to consider that. But fortunately, I do have a plan."

At this point, Bullshit-chan broke off, pointing her index finger at Umidori.

"You, Umidori."

"……………Huh?"

"If I can get your help, then I might yet extract myself from mortal peril. Oh, honest Tougetsu Umidori. You are my salvation."

"…………?"

Umidori herself was just tilting her head slowly to one side, completely lost.

"……Oh, I guess you did say something like that, Bullshit-chan. What was it? You came to me looking for a fallicide partner?

"But why me? I don't get that part at all. You've got reasons to go around killing lies; I understand that bit… But I can't see a normal high school girl like me being any help against these terrifying lies. What are you thinking, Bullshit-chan?"

"…That's where you're wrong." Bullshit-chan shook her head. "Umidori, you have a very *abnormal* talent—you cannot tell a lie."

"……Um."

Umidori locked up, blinking at her.

"Exactly, Umidori." Bullshit-chan smiled. "That's just how vital your honesty is! I came to your room today specifically to scout your unparalleled talent. To ask for the help of someone who could well become the world's greatest fallicider."

"……Again, what are you even saying, Bullshit-chan?!" Umidori wailed, her head spinning. "You're telling me that not being able to lie is a *talent*?! That this awful condition where I can only say what I actually think is somehow gonna help exterminate monsters?!"

"Heh-heh, do you not see how? I suppose you wouldn't. You're not self-aware enough to reach any other conclusion."

Umidori was looking for help, but Bullshit-chan was just blowing smoke up her ass. She was getting nowhere.

"It's totally fine if you don't get it right away. If we actually pull this fallicide off, you'll learn exactly what I mean."

"......Will I? Come on! Just tell me already!"

"Naturally, I'm not expecting you to help for free," Bullshit-chan said, ignoring the question in favor of a different subject entirely. "Eating lies to avert my death is my problem, not yours. I can hardly put you in harm's way to save myself and offer nothing in return. I fully intend to extend a reward that offsets the risk."

"......A reward? Like...money?"

"No. I mean, if you want cash, I could manage that... But I believe what I've got in mind is far more valuable to you."

Bullshit-chan flashed a grin.

"What would you do if I say helping me would enable you to lie?" she said, her voice almost a whisper.

"——Um."

"You cannot lie—you were born that way, as if cursed. A bizarre condition indeed, the likes of which no one has ever seen. I get why no doctors could help you. But, Umidori, consider this.

"The power of lies can make *anything* happen. Is that not the sole way to cure your mystery condition?"

"......Oh."

"There's nothing in this world a Beliar's wish cannot falsify, Umidori. If you are suffering from your inability to lie, then you need merely find a Beliar who will cure that condition for you."

Bullshit-chan was rattling all this off without taking a breath.

"And I'm a manifest lie who's been wandering the world of falsehoods for a decade. In that life, I've encountered any number of my kind. With me at your side, it will be no problem at all to find a Beliar capable of resolving your problem.

"This is a fair exchange, Umidori. Help me commit fallicide, and I promise to hook you up with a Beliar who can help you. I promise you will be able to lie yourself. Bullshit-chan may only lie, but rest assured, this alone is one hundred percent the truth."

"..............."

"Just imagine it, Umidori. You, lying freely. Like everyone else does. Is that not what you've always wanted?"

"......Like everyone else."

Umidori tried to imagine herself being *normal*. Lying when she wanted. Interacting with other people without anyone accusing her of not taking a hint.

"What do you say, Umidori? Will you help me murder lies?"

"...............H-hang on; my...my head's spinning. I need time to sort things out!"

"——No, I can't give you that time. I'm sorry!" Bullshit-chan said, shaking her head. "Our fallicide needs to start *now*. I'm on the ropes—and can't afford to wait for you to mull things over. If you can't make your choice here and now, I'm afraid I'll have to force you into helping me."

"......You...what? That's not right!"

"Still, I don't mind you putting off your final decision. If you decide to back out along the way, that's okay. I fully intend to respect your choice, Umidori. It would hardly be fair if you were *already* trapped."

Bullshit-chan whispered something extra ominous-sounding at the end, then turned her gaze to the door.

"Let's get this show on the road. Thanks for waiting. You can come in."

She was speaking to a third party—someone who'd been listening at the door this whole time.

"......What?"

Surprised, Umidori turned around.

And as they watched, the door swung open. Outside stood a short-haired girl in the same uniform blazer Umidori wore.

"I'm impressed you stopped yourself. I was really worried you'd barge in when I started waving the knife around!"

"Well, I figured you wouldn't actually kill her," the girl said. "And I was too busy wallowing in depression. Betrayed by a friend who insisted we were never friends at all. I didn't have it in me to fight you."

"..................Why?"

This was all Umidori could manage. Why was *she* here?

"There you have it, Umidori. This is our target—the Beliar we're after."

"Hi, Umidori. You really got me. You had me totally fooled! You're such a liar."

The girl was Yoshino Nara, and she had Tougetsu Umidori dead to rights.

Her voice betrayed no concern.

Like her expression, it was frozen stiff.

3

The Girl Named Yoshino Nara

Rumor had it Yoshino Nara was the hottest girl alive.

Not a single human on the globe was as good-looking.

No one could match her beauty.

One year ago.

On her way home from work, Umidori saw a girl sitting on a bench by the station.

The sun had already set, and it was pure coincidence that Umidori was there at all.

But the moment she saw the girl's face, she stopped in her tracks.

"……Nara."

A girl with short hair, smaller than Umidori, but wearing the same uniform blazer.

Yoshino Nara was staring into space, her face devoid of expression. She was sitting all alone on the bench, melting into the night.

"…………What's she doing here?"

Both girls had only just started high school. Umidori had yet to learn the faces of most of her classmates, but Yoshino Nara was an exception.

She was just that pretty. That had been Umidori's first impression.

When Umidori had noticed her at the entrance ceremony, her eyes locked onto those even features, despite being a girl herself.

She'd never seen anyone like Nara. Perfect eyes. A flawless nose. The ideal jawline.

Looking at her was like gazing upon a work of art—and this was hardly hyperbole. At the entrance ceremony, Umidori hadn't been the only one entranced. New students, upperclassmen, even teachers and parents all had their eyes locked and loaded on Nara. It actively disrupted the ceremony proceedings.

Here at the station, it felt like the girl's beauty was lighting up the night around her. Umidori wasn't the only one who saw it; any number of passersby were giving her very obvious looks. Still, no one was exactly causing a scene. Perhaps they couldn't fully make out her features in the darkness.

"............"

But seeing a classmate out and about was hardly remarkable. Umidori needed only pretend she hadn't seen her and walk right on by.

Talking to a classmate outside of school was a risk Umidori could not afford to take. Right now, at least, she had no intention of forming any kind of connection with anyone at all.

"——Mm?"

But as she started to turn away…

Something tugged at the edge of her vision, and she stopped her in tracks.

"..............?"

At first, she thought it was her imagination. But even in this darkness, what she'd witnessed had been all too clear—she wasn't seeing things.

Nara was always expressionless. It was impossible to tell what she was thinking. Except now. For whatever reason, a tear had rolled down her cheek.

Umidori wasn't entirely clear whether this counted as *crying*. The rest of her face was hardly scrunched up.

But from the looks of things, this wasn't nothing.

"......Uh, hey, Nara? You okay?"

The next thing she knew, Umidori was calling out to her.

This was not the outcome of any train of thought. It was pure reflex. The instant she saw that tear, Umidori completely forgot to stay out of other people's business. And before Umidori had a chance to regret that impulse, Nara's eyes turned toward her.

"...............Who are you again?"

Nara's expression didn't waver, but her voice betrayed her confusion. Registering the uniform Umidori wore, she must have assumed they were classmates.

"Oh, right, I've seen you somewhere... Class? Uh... You had an unusual name?"

"Er, um. It's Umidori. Tougetsu Umidori. *Umi* like the Sea of Japan, then the same bird as Tottori Prefecture, and the given name is *eastern moon*."

"Right, right, Umidori, okay. That stuck with me. I thought it was a pretty badass name. Especially Tougetsu—I've never heard of a girl named that."

As she spoke, Nara pulled a handkerchief out of her pocket and dried her eyes with it. Clearly, the tears had not been a product of Umidori's imagination.

"I'm Yoshino Nara. *Nara*, like Nara Prefecture. *Yoshi* is the grass radical over the character for direction, and *no* is the one that looks like a defective katana. If we're classmates, we'll be seeing each other all year, Umidori.

"So...did you come over because you thought I was sitting here cry-ing?" Nara asked, but she didn't seem especially enthused. "In that case, I should be ashamed of myself. It must have been a shock, right? Sorry, I didn't mean to drag you into my mess."

"......N-no, I'm at fault here. I saw you on your own and just came up to you. Should I have let you be?"

"Absolutely not. I really appreciate it. If you hadn't checked on me, I'd have continued that downward spiral."

Nara managed an awkward chuckle.

"...............?"

Something about the way she was acting felt wrong. Who was this girl? Why was her voice so emotional, yet her face was locked in an expression of permanent boredom?

"I mean, it wasn't anything major. I just...lost my job."

"Oh?"

"I wasn't, like, fired, exactly? The agency just said they're not going to be renewing my contract."

"......Agency?"

"Mm. I was modeling for them. I've been doing it for three years now, since my first year of junior high."

"......! G-gosh." That news got a yelp of surprise from Umidori. "I had no idea. You're a model? Wow, Nara. I guess beautiful people really do get jobs like that."

"Ha-ha, thanks. I auditioned right after entering junior high and was lucky enough to land the gig. It was a dream of mine for a long time, so I was pretty happy at the time."

"......A dream?"

"Yeah. I always wanted to be a model...," Nara whispered. The muscles in her face didn't budge, but her gaze drifted off to the distance. "I mean, I hate to say so myself, but I am pretty cute, right? I'd like to do something with the gifts I was born with. Even as a kid, I thought that much. Just like how kids who are good in gym class try to be athletes, or kids who can draw want to become manga artists. Trying for a career in show business seemed like the logical choice. Didn't really put much thought into it...," she admitted, sounding a bit bashful.

But no blush appeared on her cheeks.

"When I first started working, I got a pretty good reception. The president even said, 'We landed a real winner!' I got a bit cocky, like, See, this is what I was meant to do."

"......? Then why did they end your contract?" Umidori asked, baffled.

Nara let that hang a beat, then answered, her voice flat.

"......Pretty simple. I didn't actually sell. Three years with them, and I barely landed any jobs. Last year, I didn't get a single one. No one else on contract fared anywhere near that bad, so I can't really argue I don't deserve this. The fact that they kept me on their roster as long as they did speaks volumes to how nice everyone there was."

"......? Wh-what? But why?"

The explanation simply didn't make sense to Umidori.

"Nara, how could you not be a great model? You're so beautiful!"

"Ha-ha, you think so? That's the thing, Umidori. My beauty actually worked against me."

"......It did?"

"Basically, I'm *too* good-looking. Better-looking than any clothes our world has."

Her face blank, she spat her words.

"Every designer out there took one look at my face and swore they'd never let me wear any of their outfits. They begged my agency not to let that happen. It's a model's job to make the clothes they wear look good—and there's nothing worse than a model outshining the outfit. They all knew if a girl like me wore their designs, they'd be turned into shabby rags."

"...............Huh?"

Umidori could not believe what she was hearing.

"Wh-what the hell? You're too hot to get work? Even as a model?"

"And the same problems cropped up in other lines of work. If I try to act, there's no scripts good enough for me. If I try to sing, I rise above the songs. '*You may be the most beautiful girl in this entire profession, but we could never find a stage worthy of you. I'm so sorry.*' When the agency president says that, how am I supposed to argue?"

Nara let out a long sigh.

"If this is how it's gonna end, I should never have gone into this line of work. Pretty cute, my ass. I've always underestimated myself—a bad habit."

"..............."

Though Nara's statement was rather arrogant on the surface, it left Umidori speechless.

She'd never come across anyone who'd dream of calling themselves the most beautiful girl around. But what really boggled her mind was that as wild as Nara's statement was, she couldn't disagree with her.

Yoshino Nara was just that extraordinarily attractive.

"Well, no use crying over spilled milk. I have to move on. Umidori, did you have any plans?"

"Huh?"

"Would you care to join me for dinner?"

"...............Huh?"

Talk about a sudden twist.

It was so sudden, in fact, that Umidori froze, unable to respond.

"I just don't feel like going straight home tonight. I thought maybe eating something really good would help. Would you join me?"

"......F-for dinner? You and me?"

"There's a good *okonomiyaki* place nearby. I'm sure you'd like it. Come with!"

"............! Er, um..."

The more Nara pressed her, the more Umidori squirmed.

"......Uh, sorry, Nara. I'm glad you invited me, but I'm not sure..."

"Not sure? Why not?"

Not batting an eye, Nara crooked her head.

"Not an *okonomiyaki* fan?"

"......No, I'm not a picky eater, just..."

"You need to get home early?"

"......No, nothing like that."

"Then do you have other plans?"

"............No other plans, either."

Her voice soft and faltering, Umidori kept answering. She didn't want to get involved with other people and would have loved to give some excuse to get out of this, but...that wasn't an option to someone incapable of lying. But turning down an invitation without a reason might also create friction. Accepting the invite was out of the question, but that didn't mean she wanted to leave bad blood between her and someone she'd have to share a class with for the rest of the year.

"——I don't get it, but if you have no other plans, then you're coming with me. C'mon!"

"Augh!"

Though Umidori was at her wit's end, Nara simply reached out and grabbed her wrist—with a viselike grip.

"H-hey, Nara! Um, I really can't—"

"Ha-ha, don't worry, Umidori. It's my treat. I might have been an unsuccessful model, but I've got enough saved up to buy dinner for a classmate."

"I-it's not a question of money! I'm really bad at these things! Please, listen to me, Nara!"

——That was how Tougetsu Umidori and Yoshino Nara first met.

Their connection survived the year, gradually building something that could be called a rapport. Until…

◇◇◇◇

She took out a frying pan.

A standard steel pan, not that deep, fairly wide. The kind you could find at any store, totally unremarkable. Its surface was free of stains or nicks—it had likely gone almost entirely unused.

"Last night, I received a message," Yoshino Nara said, flicking the flat of the frying pan with her finger a few times, then putting it down on the burner. "'Are you aware that someone has been stealing your pencils for a year now?' it said. 'If you think I'm making this up, test it. Leave a mark on the pencils that only you can identify.'"

Nara pulled a bottle off the shelf, full of a yellowish translucent fluid. It was vegetable oil, and the label read, HEALTHY! PERFECT FOR SALADS.

"The sender was unknown. The name of the account was Bullshit-chan, which was obviously unserious. I assumed it was some sort of chain-letter scam. That said, there was no downside in actually testing the idea; I figured it would kill some time, at least, and gave it a shot. And lo and behold…the mark I left actually did disappear."

Nara sighed, but her face remained blank. She unscrewed the lid on the bottle and tilted it over the stove, slowly pouring oil into the pan.

"But I figured the odds were very high this Bullshit-chan *wasn't* the Pencil Thief. After all, why would someone who'd spent a year taking pains to prevent me ever catching on to their crimes suddenly reveal themselves like this? It made no sense. So when we talked in class, Umidori, I didn't mention her—I acted like I'd figured this all out on my own, trying to deduce who the Pencil Thief really was."

Glop, glop. The pan slowly filled with yellowish oil.

When it was one-third full, Nara righted the bottle and replaced the cap. Then she switched on the burner, heating the oil in the pan on high.

"Right after I left school, I got another message from Bullshit-chan.

A single sentence. 'I'm right behind you.' I may have yelped. No, it was a straight-up scream.

"I slowly turned around and found a white-haired girl in a cat-ear hoodie. Bit of a letdown!"

"Meanwhile, I was freaking out," Bullshit-chan said, standing to one side. "I'd known Nara was supposed to be ridiculously beautiful, but up close, she really took my breath away. People this good-looking really do exist!"

"I think your behavior is far more ridiculous. I asked your real name and school, and you just made up stuff." Nara shrugged, sounding skeptical. "But I guess there's not much else to explain. I followed this mystery kid here—to the lair of the Pencil Thief. She barged in first, and I sneaked in after—and stood outside the toilet stall with my ear to the door."

Another minute had passed as she was talking. Nara held her palm over the frying pan, checking the temperature of the oil. She let a few more seconds go by in silence, then nodded and turned around.

"When I first opened the fridge door, I nearly passed out. All these pencils, shaved to half-length, stuffed in there—it was all I could do not to puke. But the anger overwhelmed the fear. I wanted nothing more than to punch the thief in the face."

"——That urge eventually passed, at the exact moment I heard the last voice I ever expected coming out of that stall."

Nara had turned to the fridge.

She opened the door, grabbed a few of the pencils within, and took them out. She turned back to the kitchen, standing in front of the stove again.

Then she threw the entire handful of pencils into the frying pan.

"Noooooooooooooooooo!"

A scream went up behind Nara.

It had escaped the lips of one Tougetsu Umidori, watching the scene like the very world was ending.

"Noooooooooooo! Doooooon't! How could you do that to my poor pencils?!"

She staggered toward the stove, reaching for Nara's shoulders—but Nara brusquely brushed her off.

"Shut the hell up! They're not your pencils; they're mine!"

Nara's face betrayed none of the fury in her tone.

"Fry, fry, fry, fry 'em all! Take that! And that!"

It was hard to believe such a powerful roar could come out of that tiny body. She yanked open the kitchen drawer, grabbed some silicon cooking chopsticks, and started turning the pencils in the oil.

"No! Stop! No more! Why are you cooking them through?! Those are loaded with fingerprints! You're sterilizing them!"

Umidori clapped her hands to her eyes, unable to watch. She knelt where she stood. Nara didn't even bother to glance at her. She just stomped back to the fridge.

"Augh, to hell with it! I'm throwing them all in!" she snapped, and with both hands, she grabbed as many pencils as she could. "Hoo-hah!"

With a shout, she swung back to the stove and tried to fling both handfuls of pencils into the frying pan. Just before that happened, however, Umidori vaulted up, putting Nara in a full nelson.

"W-wait! S-s-s-stop, Nara! That's legit dangerous! You don't wanna do that!"

"Sh-shut up! Let go of me, pencil pervert! I'm gonna flip if anything this messed up exists a second longer! I'm gonna fry them all! I'm making pencil tempura!"

The two high school girls grappled over the frying pan. But where Umidori's face twisted in desperation, Yoshino Nara's expression never once shifted.

"Uh, okay, both of you calm down! Fighting over hot oil will not end well! And you can't make tempura without any breading! This is just normal deep-frying!"

Bullshit-chan was offering important rebuttals, but nobody was listening.

And a second later…

"——?! Ah! Aiiiiiieeee!"

…an extra piercing shriek left Umidori's lips.

She had seen a change come over the hundred-odd pencils in the frying pan.

Even in hot vegetable oil, the pencils themselves were wood—they weren't taking much damage. The problem was the outside.

The paint on the surface of that wood was peeling away as the temperature rose.

"Noooooooo! That's the most important paaaaart! That's what Nara's fingers touched the mooooooost!"

Umidori staggered and swooned, her last shred of morale gone. Given the original color of the pencil paint, the remnants of it floating in the oil looked rather like vegetables frying.

◇◇◇◇

"——Whew, my bad. Got a little carried away there."

All three girls were sitting on the floor around the table.

Yoshino Nara.

Tougetsu Umidori.

And Bullshit-chan—although she might not technically be a "girl."

The digital clock on the table showed six. Evening had arrived. That said, it was April—there was still light out beyond those closed curtains, but the mood in the room remained dark.

"I was so worked up I couldn't rein in my emotions until I had disposed of every last pencil. I'm glad the frying plan worked out. I can't imagine how poorly this would have gone if you hadn't happened to own an untouched bottle of vegetable oil."

"Yes, what a coincidence. Umidori just happened to purchase a bottle of oil when she first started living alone, then left it on the shelf without using a drop of it.

"Still, it was quite a spectacle, Nara. I had no idea what deep-frying pencils would look like! It was like a science experiment. Such fun!"

"I wasn't doing it to entertain you. But at the very least, disposing of those pencils is some small comfort."

"................."

Nara and Bullshit-chan were exchanging pleasantries, but Umidori was sitting in silence, as if her soul had left her body. A worrying degree of color had drained from her face, and her head was down. Her knees had finally stopped buckling, and now her eyes had clouded over. No signs of life.

"——Still, just because the pencil incident is solved doesn't mean I can dust off my hands and go home. After all, your toilet conversation informed me that I am mixed up in a matter every bit as bizarre, one I can hardly believe is a part of the world in which I live."

Nara turned her gaze toward the girl in the cat-ear hoodie.

"Bullshit-chan, with the pencils safely disposed of, I think it's time we addressed that concern. Let me summarize the salient points of your speech. The lies we humans regularly tell are actually living creatures. You are a lie made manifest and need to consume other such manifest lies. To do so, you need to deal with the lie's host, or Beliar, and I am one of these Belied."

"Yes, that understanding is completely correct, Nara," Bullshit-chan said, her smiling unwavering. "I'm glad our conversation was audible through the door."

"That said, I didn't find your explanation particularly helpful," Nara told her, scratching her cheek. "I mean, you say I'm a Beliar, but I have no idea what that even means."

"............Hmph."

Bullshit-chan merely snorted. A loaded sort of snort.

"Meaning?" she asked.

"Well, I don't want to directly contradict your assertation, but I don't see how I, Yoshino Nara, could possibly be a Beliar. After all, until I heard your explanation, I was completely unaware of the existence of these creatures you call lies."

Nara's face remained a blank slate, but her voice bore distinct signs of befuddlement.

"At the very least, I have never seen the manifest lie allegedly possessing me. For that reason, I find it difficult to accept your accusation. There has to be some kind of mistake."

"No, there is no mistake, Nara," Bullshit-chan declared, her gaze as intent as Nara's. "You see, lies give off an odor, if you will, that only those of their own kind can detect. This fauxroma is very distinctive."

"Fauxroma?"

"The stench of it is wafting off your body even as we speak, Nara. An ultra-powerful stink that likes of which I have almost never encountered. As long as my nose is detecting that, there is no doubt whatsoever that you are an extremely strong Beliar."

"......Ew, that's horrible."

It didn't show on her face, but Nara's voice sounded aghast.

"A fauxroma... The idea that something like that is wafting off me makes me sick."

"It's not really worth worrying about. No human is odor-free, and I'm a lie myself, so it's not a particularly noxious scent."

"Maybe it doesn't bother you, but it does me! I'm at the end of my rope here. I want to rid myself of this uncanny stench as soon as possible."

"......Huh, that's your goal?" Bullshit-chan said, frowning. "Just to be absolutely clear, Nara, are you sure you don't mind?"

"Mind what?"

"I mean, getting rid of the lie, going along with my fallicide, that means..."

Here, Bullshit-chan visibly hesitated.

"I'll be eating the lie you've told. Your wish won't come true."

"Oh, that's perfectly fine," Nara said, not even hesitating. "Knock yourself out. Frankly, the idea of my lie coming true is downright terrifying."

"......Terrifying?"

"Listen, Bullshit-chan, I don't even *have* a desire I want granted. At best, I think it would be cool to win the lottery? So if a lie I've told is made manifest, that means my *unconsciousness* is making it happen. This desire lies somewhere deep down, and I'm not even aware of it.

"And that idea is simply alarming. Bullshit-chan, I don't want my sub-conscious altering the very world. If, deep down, I'm harboring a wish for world destruction, and this might actually come to pass? Even though the part of me I am aware of doesn't want anything like that at all?"

Nara shrugged blankly.

"So I don't need a lie. I don't want one possessing me. If you'd like to eat my lie, I'll happily help you out. Honestly, I think it's a shame I can't get rid of it myself."

"......Ah-ha."

Bullshit-chan was watching Nara's face closely, but since it never changed at all, this required extremely meticulous observation.

"Well, if you say so, Nara, then that works for me."

"So how, specifically, do we go about committing fallicide? This girl who can't lie and hasn't said a word in several minutes? I believe you suggested getting her to do something about me."

"..................."

Umidori had not joined their conversation at all. Her head was still down, and her soul was nowhere to be seen.

"......Yes, good point, I should really explain that part."

Bullshit-chan took a breath and launched into her next speech.

"Hear me, Nara—and you, Umidori. You've both been dismissive about her inability to lie, but to my eyes, you are grossly underestimating just how powerful an ability that is—nothing can more easily move the human heart."

"......How so?"

"I'll admit, verbal explanations won't suffice. Let us try a demonstration instead. Umidori."

"......Mm?"

She hadn't been expecting her name, and she looked up in surprise. Bullshit-chan gave her a plaintive look.

"I am sorry, Umidori. I made the call to reveal your darkest secrets to Nara. I genuinely regret it. I solemnly swear I'll never do that again."

"......Huh? Wh-where'd that come from?"

The heartfelt apology just rattled Umidori... But a moment later, a mischievous grin took over Bullshit-chan's face.

"See? Just now, I apologized—but did Umidori forgive me? Of course not! It's easy to *say* I'm sorry, but she has no way of telling if I really mean that."

Bullshit-chan shook her head emphatically.

"But if I were like Umidori and incapable of lying? In that case, if I said '*I'm sorry*' then that is a verifiable truth! It means I am genuinely remorseful! Umidori has a kind heart, so that alone would be enough to earn her forgiveness. Even though I'd only offered a verbal apology.

"On the other hand, what if I wasn't actually repentant? In that case, I couldn't say sorry at all. I'd be forced to admit that I didn't actually regret it. And that would only serve to fan the flames of Umidori's anger."

"......Ah-ha," Nara said, sounding convinced. "So her condition has upsides and downsides."

"I'm glad you understand. My point is—the inability to lie is an extremely effective means of churning people's emotions and *persuading* them. Ordinarily, shaking someone from their position requires a Herculean effort—for the simple reason that you humans all view mere words as largely empty. Because you're all liars.

"But Umidori is incapable of uttering empty words. Her words cut people to the quick. If she says she loves someone, then she loves them from the bottom of her heart. If she says she despises them, then that rancor is festering.

"Her inability to lie works for her and against her. It's a double-edged sword. A candor claymore, if you will."

"......A candor claymore."

"But Umidori's life thus far has left her all too conscious of the claymore's downsides. She has utterly failed to take advantage of the benefits. She's made no effort to involve herself with others and has actively pushed people away using what she calls *techniques*. She's applied those thoroughly to achieve a fragile peace.

"And that's exactly why I had to corner Umidori and position her where she was unable to apply those techniques. Do something to her she never saw coming—like reveal the secret she'd kept hidden all this while. I knew she wouldn't be able to keep a level head or, at the very least, no longer have the leeway to stop herself from getting *involved*."

"..............Do you mean"—Umidori's voice shook—"that's the whole reason you told Nara I was the Pencil Thief?!"

"——Basically, yes." Bullshit-chan nodded, smiling. "See, Umidori? Now you don't need to handle Nara with kid gloves. You're past the point of worrying your head about trifles like whether you're too closely involved. If you ask me, this will make you much happier."

"..............."

"So don't give me that baleful glare. I do apologize for tricking you into spilling the beans; it's definitely my fault, and I have no intention of offering excuses for my behavior." Bullshit-chan's voice took on a mocking lilt. "I mean, if she wasn't a friend, what do you care if she's disillusioned?"

"..............!"

Umidori flinched and hung her head. That was an argument she couldn't refute.

"But I'm not a monster. I don't expect you to start committing fallicide right away."

Bullshit-chan was smiling, but she was paying close attention to Umidori's responses.

"We need you to settle down first. How about we take a break and get some food?"

"......Food?"

"Yes, I mean, look at the clock. It's dinnertime! You're both too hungry to focus on murdering lies. It's high time we refilled our energy tanks. Don't you humans have an expression along the lines of 'You can't fight on an empty stomach?'"

".........Um." This suggestion just seemed to baffle Umidori. "I—I don't... Food? There's some rice in the cooker, but that's really all I've got..."

"Oh, that's what you're worried about? Don't be; I've got this handled."

Way ahead of Umidori, Bullshit-chan puffed up her modest chest.

"I'm actually a pretty good cook! And if you're lacking in ingredients, that's nothing a quick trip to the grocery store won't solve."

"...........Huh?" This seemed to shock Umidori more than anything else. "Th-the grocery story? You're going, Bullshit-chan? Now?"

"Yes! You two wait right here. I'll be back in half an hour!"

"...........H-half an hour..."

Umidori was screaming inside. Being alone with Nara for that long would be pure torture. "I-I'll come with!"

"No need. I'm not a child; I can handle a little shopping on my own."

"B-but shopping for three could get heavy! A-and do you even have money, Bullshit-chan?"

"Of course I do," Bullshit-chan said, pulling an adorable bifold wallet out of her hoodie pocket. It had a cat embroidered on it. "See? And to make up for all the trouble I caused, this one's entirely on me. Don't worry about a thing!"

"——?! Wh-why do you have that? You're not human, Bullshit-chan!"

"Ha-ha-ha, Umidori, I *look* human. And that alone means there's any number of ways to legally acquire currency."

Cackling, she put the wallet away.

"Over the decade I've spent blending into your world, I've learned that there are advantages to carrying around cash. And because I'm not human, I can easily carry enough food for three. I won't be requiring any assistance."

"..............!"

"There you have it, Umidori. Sit back and enjoy your first-ever bedroom date with Nara! See you in thirty!"

And with that last bombshell, Bullshit-chan actually *did* leave.

"................."

"................."

A hellish silence settled over the room.

Neither Umidori nor Nara moved so much as a muscle. Umidori couldn't have moved even if she'd wanted to. They were physically in close proximity, but that only served to amplify how thoroughly awkward things were.

What was Nara thinking? Umidori kept one eye on her, wondering. But Nara's expression betrayed nothing, and she was not looking at Umidori—it was impossible to fathom her emotions. Ordinarily, she was pretty talkative, but once she clammed up like this, it instantly became impossible to read her mind.

Umidori would have loved to jump to her feet and flee the room right this instant. How had she wound up in this predicament? It wasn't that long ago she'd been thoroughly enjoying a meal made from Nara's pencils. The height of luxury.

——Then out of nowhere...

"——!"

Umidori's phone vibrated in the pocket of her skirt. Surprised, she reached into her pocket, taking it out. Someone had sent her a message.

".........?" Only a few people even knew Umidori's address. And the only person she regularly exchanged messages with was Nara. So who was this? She tried to check the sender—

"——Eep?!"

—but let out a shriek, the phone falling to the floor.

She was in no state to hold on to it.

The instant her gaze had turned to her hand, Nara had abruptly flung her arms around Umidori.

"Huh? Huh? Wh-what?"

"……………"

Nara wasn't answering.

Wordlessly, she just gave Umidori a long, hard squeeze. Given the difference in their relative sizes, that left Nara's face buried in the valley between Umidori's breasts.

"……Umidori," Nara said, her voice muffled. "Do you even get what I'm so mad about?"

"……Um?" A direct question, but all Umidori could do was stare at the top of Nara's head, perplexed. "Er, um… What's going on? Why are you hugging me?"

"Huh? What, am I not allowed to hug you now?"

Nara seemed inexplicably infuriated.

"Spare me your protests and answer the question! I'm sure you know by now that I'm thoroughly pissed off! I've totally lost my shit! But do you actually understand what, specifically, has gotten me so worked up?!"

"……Er, um." To Umidori, this was all coming out of nowhere, and the quiver in her voice betrayed that. "W-well, I've kind of said everything. I was stealing your pencils behind your back, then eating them with rice, which is inherently creepy—"

"That's not it at all."

"—It isn't?"

"That answer is completely and utterly wrong. I'm appalled, Umidori. What an incredibly stupid misapprehension.

"How little you must think of me, Umidori. You have a niche fetish for eating fingerprints, and you made me a target of it. And so what? That would never make me turn against you."

"………………Huh?"

Nara had said that so emphatically Umidori could only squeak in response.

"Wh-what? How does that work? You're not mad about the pencils?"

"I'll say it as many times as you like. I don't care one goddamn bit about that, and I'm not mad at you for hiding all that from me, either. I'm well aware that was not something you could easily share.

"……So I got over it. I've forgiven you for it, Umidori."

Nara's voice took on a tinge of sadness.

"I am not mad because you were the Pencil Thief. What I can't get past...is you insisting that we weren't friends."

"——Hmm?"

"How can you possibly claim we weren't that close?! That's just mean! I almost fainted on the spot when I heard you say that!

"We've spent a year as classmates. I thought we had a lot of fun together! But to you, I was nothing but a means to indulge in your base urges. Was that it?!"

"..............."

"We're high school students. I'm, like, the only person still using pencils! My mind's still rejecting the idea. I was so comfortable spending time with you, but that whole time, you were just putting up with me? You didn't even like me! You just wanted to eat my fingerprints!"

"......Nara," Umidori gasped, eyes locked on Nara's tiny head.

"You are such an idiot, Umidori. I'm never letting you off the hook for this. I hope you ate so many pencils that you wind up in the hospital with graphite poisoning."

"............"

Squeeeeeeeeeze...... Nara's embrace was only getting tighter, and Umidori was left searching for words in vain.

She'd never once seen Nara acting like this.

No matter how depressed she got, she'd never once sounded this sad.

She'd never once clung to Umidori like a little kid.

"I-I'm sorry, Nara. What I said really hurt you. It was thoughtless," Umidori managed after quite a long time. "But...give me a second; I have something I want to add."

"......What?"

"I don't mean this as an excuse. But I do think you've misunderstood some things."

"..............?"

Nara peeled her head out from between Umidori's breasts, looking up at her, expressionless.

"It's true that I've never once thought you were my friend." Umidori nodded. "That wasn't a lie."

"......Yes, you said."

"——But I didn't say I don't like you."

"......Huh?"

"I don't remember ever saying I didn't like you, Nara."

Umidori was very emphatic.

But no sooner had the words left her mouth than her eyes had started swimming.

"But even so, it's still true I've never considered us friends, so..."

"......What does that mean?"

"Nara, you're closer to me than any other girl has ever been. At all my previous schools, I was always alone. I never had anyone else I could just have regular chitchat with.

"So having you sitting next to me and getting to shoot the breeze with you—that meant a lot. The way you'd keep a poker face while cracking wild jokes—*comfortable*'s a good word, yeah. I wished it wasn't just in class! I'd have loved to hang out in town or in each other's rooms. I mean, the pencil thing meant inviting you here, and that was never a feasible option..."

"......But you still didn't consider me your friend."

"......No." Umidori nodded. "I mean, it seemed like you thought I was your friend."

"..............Huh?"

"And if we both thought of the other as friends, then that means we *are* friends! That means we're *too close*. Any careless word I said could hurt you, and I was scared of that—so I clammed up. I couldn't let myself think of you as a friend."

"...........Umidori."

"I was so alone," Umidori whispered. "I never fit in at school. I was desperate for friends, but I could never make any. Yet I still felt lonely, so I kept trying to involve myself somehow, and that led to—"

"...........To stealing pencils?" Nara said, finally starting to catch on. "Eating fingerprints was a proxy action, replacing your inability to be social normally?"

"......Eating fingerprints wasn't *actually* interacting with anyone. I was well aware of that! And no matter how many pencils I ate, I didn't get any less miserable. But it did distract from my loneliness."

".............."

"As I grew older, my pencil-swapping escapades got more and more infrequent. I know replacing other people's things is wrong! I didn't steal a single pencil in my third year of junior high.

"But in high school, I met you and slipped back into my old habits. Before I knew it, I was shaving your pencils onto rice for dinner. That made it feel like I was interacting with you like *friends*... And yeah, I know how stupid that is."

Umidori's voice deflated.

"So when I say I like you, Nara, that's definitely true. I wouldn't steal a friend's pencils, but I definitely wouldn't steal pencils from someone I didn't even like."

".............."

".............."

".............."

".............Um, so how long are you gonna hug me, Nara?" Umidori asked after an extended awkward silence. "I-it's been a really long time, and you're kind of embarrassing me..."

"......Mm, right," Nara said, only to immediately bury her face in Umidori's bosom again. "I would very much like to let go, but I don't think that's going to be possible anytime soon."

"Oh? Um, why?"

"Having my face buried in your boobs feels way too good, and I can't let go."

".........Huh?"

"I just hugged you on impulse, but it was far more dangerous than anticipated." Nara sounded extremely earnest. "They're so big! So soft! Once you nestle in between them, it's impossible to extract yourself! Your boobs work on the same principle as the *kotatsu*."

"......?! Uh, um, Nara...are you listening to yourself?!"

Umidori had turned bright red.

"I thought you were burrowing in there, but I'd rather not hear any weird reviews! Boobs and *kotatsu* have nothing in common!"

"I've wondered what this felt like for quite some time, actually. But we never met anywhere outside of school, and I felt it would be inappropriate to request this in class! I've been waiting for the right opportunity—and at last, it presented itself! This alone was well worth the trip to your apartment.

"——Come to think of it, when I was outside the bathroom listening to you and Bullshit-chan, there was a lot of shocking revelations. You being the Pencil Thief, Bullshit-chan not being human, me being this Beliar thing—but your measurements were every bit as shocking! Your bust is thirty-nine inches?! What are you, a pinup model?!"

"......! D-don't tease me about it, Nara! I'm just tall and gain weight faster than most people, and I'm not a fan of it!"

"......Puh-leeze. What are you talking about, Umidori? Your build is what makes you so attractive!"

Nara let out an exasperated sigh.

"You really don't get it. Not just your physical attractiveness, but how appealing you are on the inside, too."

"Huh?"

"I bet you don't have a clue how much I really care about you."

She sounded like a sulky child.

"......Nara?"

"......It's so not fair, Umidori. This candor claymore thing! 'I've never thought of her as a friend!' A horrible betrayal! I want to hold it against you a lot longer, but then you say you like me, and I know I have to believe you! It just brings immediate relief, like, 'Oh, I was right, she *does* like me back.'"

Nara sounded deeply bitter, like someone nursing a vendetta.

"By the way, Umidori, do you remember when we first met?"

"Huh?"

"April of last year, when you came up to me on the bench by the station."

"......Um, yes, I remember that." Umidori nodded. "We went out for *okonomiyaki*, right?"

"Yes, we did. We both ordered *modanyaki*. It was very good."

"......Oh? Uh, I guess I don't remember the specific order."

"I remember everything."

This was clearly taking Nara back.

"After all, that was the first time I'd ever been so upset I cried in front of anyone."

"......Oh."

Umidori thought back to that single tear running down Nara's poker face.

"That night has stuck with me ever since. Even at the counter in the *okonomiyaki* shop, I was still dragging it around with me, but you kept trying to cheer me up."

"......? I—I did?"

Umidori did her best to remember, but it had happened a year ago. She recalled finding Nara at the station—that had been memorable. But she couldn't summon up anything they'd talked about at the restaurant.

"Ha-ha, sounds like you've forgotten most of it. Maybe consoling someone isn't that memorable. But having you call out to me and sit with me that day really saved me."

"Oh?"

"I didn't give you the full rundown, but I was super serious about the modeling thing. I did everything in my power to make my dream come true—to no avail. Three years of work, and they just gave me the ax. I was really in the dumps. Totally broken up about it."

Her voice grew bleak merely recounting this.

"But then you were there for me, and that got me going again. If I'd been alone that night, I'd have cried myself to sleep. But instead, it became a happy *okonomiyaki* memory. I can't thank you enough for it, really."

"......I—I don't know what to say. I just let you drag me out to eat. I didn't really do anything."

"If that's how you see it, fine. I just wanna say this"—Nara's voice was soft, like she was trying to reason with an unruly child—"I am in your camp so deep that no matter how weird your fetish is, it will never turn me against you. Don't you ever forget that, no matter what other problems you're dealing with."

"...........Nara."

"——So enough about that!"

Nara patted Umidori gently on the shoulder, then peeled her face away from her ample bosom and stood up.

"I won't bring up the Pencil Thief thing again. We've officially made up. Water under the bridge! Let's refocus on this fallicide business."

She matched this proclamation with, as always, no discernable expression. The same old Yoshino Nara, just as Umidori knew her.

"Oh, right, if we're eating together, I'd better call home and let them know I won't need dinner."

"......Huh? Oh, right, maybe."

"I'll just pop outside and call them. Won't be long."

With that, Nara headed to the door. Umidori watched her go, then let out a long, relieved sigh.

"...............Whew."

Looking rather dazed, she stared down at her own chest. It was like she could still feel Nara's beautiful face nestled in her valley, like her warmth still lingered. It went without saying this was the first time Umidori had ever been hugged by a girl from her class.

"..............."

And as she savored Nara's warmth, she ran back through everything she'd said, chewing it all over.

"......I've thought this before, but she's an odd duck. Most people wouldn't even consider hugging a creepy pencil-eating thief."

And in class, she'd sounded quite appalled by the thief's actions.

Even now, it wasn't like she'd indicated she understood the act of eating pencils in any way.

Just knowing that the unsettling Pencil Thief was Tougetsu Umidori had been all she needed to move past it.

"......If Nara and I are *actually* friends now, I'm super, super, super excited."

Umidori tried to picture it.

Going out together after school, hanging out in each other's rooms on weekends, spending time with the girl who sat next to her like normal friends did.

As long as Umidori couldn't lie, however, this was just a daydream.

"......But if I learn to lie, maybe it won't be."

"There's nothing in this world a Beliar's wish cannot falsify, Umidori. If you are suffering from your inability to lie, then you need merely find a Beliar who will cure that condition for you."

......But was that actually possible? Umidori wasn't inclined to trust anything Bullshit-chan said. For that matter, she still hadn't fully wrapped her head around the concept of lies falsifying the world.

But even then—if there was a chance she could learn to lie, even a 1 percent chance...

Then it might be worth helping Bullshit-chan with her so-called fallicide.

......Still, Umidori really didn't get the logic behind the whole "her inability to lie will help murder lies" thing.

"......Oh, right."

This train of thought reminded her of something.

Just before Nara hugged Umidori, her phone had vibrated; she'd gotten a message. Since Umidori had dropped the phone on the floor, she hadn't actually read it yet.

Who'd sent this to her anyway? Curious, Umidori reached down and picked up the phone.

"...............Uh."

When she saw the sender's name, she let out a wheeze.

It read: Bullshit-chan.

"......How does she have my contact info?"

Baffled, Umidori opened the message, assuming Bullshit-chan was asking how she and Nara were getting along. Or perhaps something she'd forgotten to explain about the fallicide process.

"...........Huh?"

But when the message opened, Umidori's eyes jumped to a phrase she'd hadn't anticipated.

The very first line read:

Don't trust Yoshino Nara. She's lying to you.

◇◇◇◇

Nara is our enemy.

Best to assume that and act accordingly.

Allow me to explain.

Yes, Nara indicated a willingness to help us kill lies. She acted like an ally.

But, Umidori—that is almost certainly a lie.

Did none of that ring false? It's unconscious? Her subconscious is falsifying the world?

Indeed, Umidori. Ain't no way.

An unconscious lie could never be that powerful. How could it?

Nara knows exactly what we're talking about.

She's hell-bent on deceiving us.

She's been told the wish she's long held could come true. And so, she's going to do everything in her power to make that happen.

Nara is not trying to kill the lie she's telling; she's trying to kill me.

She believes she'll be in the clear if she can feign ignorance until my life runs out.

That means we have to finish off Nara's lie before I meet my demise.

Which means we have to figure it out.

What lie is Yoshino Nara telling?

If we can discern that, we've as good as won.

If we know what she wants, what her desire is, it'll be easy to murder that thought.

Right now, we can make some big assumptions.

It almost certainly centers on her appearance.

Nara's beauty is exceptional. She's downright unnecessarily hot.

And any trait that exaggerated creates frictions in life—how does she feel about her looks?

Consider that well.

Speculate around that point.

If you find the answer, I'm sure you can kill that lie.

……One last thing, Umidori.

One thing I need to make absolutely, positively clear.

We have to murder Nara's lie.

Defeat is not an option. We cannot even dream of escaping.

Why? Because she's a Beliar.

She's fucked in the head.

She's a major threat.

No matter how rational she tries to act, she cannot fool me. Everything about Nara is exactly like the sinister Belied I've faced before.

Beliars are evil. The enemies of the world.

I know better than anyone how terrifying they can be.

We cannot let her roam free.

……But I know saying all this may not convince you, Umidori. Whatever the shape of it, you and Nara have been together for over a year.

I barely know the girl, and I know that means nothing I say will bear much weight.

But think about it, Umidori.

How well do you really know Nara?

Do you know what kind of life she's led? How her values might have changed? I imagine you haven't the slightest clue.

Can you truly tell me she's rational? Not the tiniest bit crazy? Not dangerous in the least?

Right. You can't.

You see, Umidori?

You don't know the first thing about Nara.

4

Young and Old, Male and Female

"What's wrong, Umidori?"

——A voice from the door made Umidori jump.

"..............!"

She spun around to face the speaker. As she did, she put her phone into sleep mode and slid it under the round table.

"I really caught you by surprise, huh? Doom scrolling some particularly shocking news?"

The speaker—Yoshino Nara—was taking off her shoes. She didn't sound especially interested.

"Oh, my parents are okay with it. It's Friday, after all. They said I'm free to stay for dinner and spend the night if I want.

"They also said to thank your parents or guardian. Heh-heh, I bet even my mom wouldn't be quite so laissez-faire if she knew her kid was spending the night somewhere without any adult supervision. I figured that would just throw a wrench in the whole thing, so I left that part out."

Nara shrugged, stalked across the room, and joined Umidori at the table.

"Hokay."

"............"

Umidori was in no state to hear a word Nara was saying.

Her mind was stuffed to the brim with the contents of Bullshit-chan's message.

Nara is our enemy.
She's hell-bent on deceiving us.
"......Um, Umidori? You with me? You've turned super pale. I'm not kidding!"
"——Huh?"
"What, did Bullshit-chan send you some critical new info on lies?"
".................?!"
Nara tossed that out, and Umidori utterly failed to cover, visibly flinching.
"..............Huh? H-how'd you know?"
".............."
Nara didn't answer.
She just gave Umidori a long, expressionless look.
"......Nah, doesn't really matter," she said after a very long silence. She let out a breath, slumping.

"More importantly, Umidori, there's something I want to share with you."

"......Oh?"
Startled, Umidori swiveled her eyes toward Nara.
"......There is?"
"Yeah. I mean, it's nothing major. Just a little history."
"......History?"
"Yep. My past." Nara nodded to herself. "While I was on the phone, my brain kinda caught up with me. Given all that's going on, I think you deserve to know."
"......Okay?"
"For one thing, I'm not the kind of girl who lets someone else set the pace. It's high time I took charge—I always do."
"......??"
"Umidori, not to drop a bombshell on you...," Nara said, not waiting for Umidori's go-ahead. "But I'm really pretty."
"...........Yes?"
"I'm a bit too pretty, if I do say so myself. It's downright scary that anyone as beautiful as I am is actually allowed to exist.

"......But sometimes it makes me wonder. Wonder at the very fact that I was born this good-looking. I come from a totally ordinary family. I'm a thoroughly normal girl. So why is the shape of my face alone this perfect? Did the stars align? Is this a blessing fit for a totally average girl like me?

"What do you make of it, Umidori? Why am I this hot?"

"...............?"

Umidori had no clue what to say. She just blinked at Nara.

"......Um, I—I really don't know. I assumed you've got a pretty face because your parents' genes just happened to combine well."

"That's not the least bit true, Umidori," Nara declared. "This is *not* a coincidence. Human faces do not get aligned this beautifully without a reason or a cause. It's simple logic."

"......Huh?"

"As early as I can remember, I'd been thinking about the reason. Considering the cause every time I caught sight of myself in a mirror. Incidentally, Umidori, have you heard of noblesse oblige?"

"......? No-bless what?"

"The duty of the privileged. Those who are superior to others are obligated to use their talents and skills for the benefit of society. Someone like me was given a mission from God at the moment of my birth, and I cannot abandon that.

"And as the most beautiful girl alive, what is my mission? Given all I've said, I imagine you can guess."

"...........N-no, I'm clueless."

"I have to *share* it, just like how the wealthy are obligated to give charity to the poor. I was born prettier than anyone else, and I have a duty to distribute this beauty to everyone else."

"......Um, seriously, what are you talking about, Nara?"

Umidori was beyond mincing her words. Nara let out a disgusted sigh.

"Do you still not get it, Umidori? I am telling you about the lie I told."

She just tossed this out like it was nothing.

....

"...! ...?!?!?!"

Umidori's entire face started twitching.

"……Huh?! Huh?!"

"Still, realizing this fact did not allow me to fulfill my obligation on my own. I did the best I could all the way through junior high, but it just didn't work out. Reality is a harsh mistress. The world we live in rejected my contributions."

Nara continued to deliver her speech, seemingly oblivious to Umidori's reactions.

"I lost hope. I forgot all about my mission and resigned myself to living like any other high school girl. The impulse still smolders within me—I'm barely keeping a lid on it. I mean, no matter how much I want to fulfill that mission, I failed to make it happen. Giving up was my only choice.

"……But what if it wasn't? What if there was a power that could make dreams come true? And by some miracle, I obtained it? Safe to say I wouldn't hesitate. I'd latch on to that power and falsify the very world."

"——Get away from Nara, Umidori!"

A girl's voice.

From the door, cutting through Nara's torrent of words.

"You can't be that close to her!"

It was Bullshit-chan.

She was just inside the front entrance, supermarket bags in both hands, scowling at Nara.

"She's already—"

"That was fast, Bullshit-chan," Nara said, glancing her way. "Oh dear. I was hoping to take care of this before you got back, before you could interfere. Shame. But at least this way I only have to explain myself once."

"Nara, you can't—"

"Heh-heh, no use giving me that look now. As you can see, it's already way too late."

As Nara spoke, she raised a hand, palm out—and brought it toward Umidori's face.

"………………Huh?"

"——Accept it, Umidori. You deserve to be the first person falsified."

An instant later—

"——?!"

——searing pains shot across Umidori's face.

"O-owww?!"

She clapped her hands to her face.

"Ow, ow, ow, ow, ow...?!"

Never in her life had she felt such pain. It was overwhelming, like someone was slicing up her face with a knife. She couldn't sit still; her head dropped, and she curled up.

"I am sorry, Umidori. You'll have to endure a little pain."

Nara's calm tones floated down from above.

"But it'll only hurt at first. You should already be past it. The facelift is already complete."

"...........H-huh?!"

She had a point. The pain was no longer as strong. Hands still on her face, Umidori gingerly lifted her head.

"Come, Umidori. Take a look at your face," Nara said, pulling a mirror out of her uniform pocket. She slid it across the table. "I imagine you'll be rather surprised."

"Huh......? W-wait......"

The mirror slid off the table, falling toward her thighs, and Umidori caught it on reflex...and as she did, the folded mirror opened.

This left her looking into the glass—and she caught sight of her own face reflected in it.

"..............Huh?"

And what she saw there made her yelp in surprise.

"......?! Wh-what the...what's going on?"

She locked her eyes on the mirror, unable to tear her gaze away.

"M-my face...my face is..."

"Heh-heh, well? Pretty sweet gift, right?"

Watching Umidori's reaction closely, Nara sounded proud of herself.

"There you have it, Umidori. This is the lie I'm telling."

◇◇◇◇

"——Why don't I have expressions?" Nara repeated, sounding annoyed. But she didn't *look* annoyed.

Face frozen in place, she looked perpetually bored—and also far younger than she would in high school.

"Yes, can I get an answer?"

At the receiving end of her gaze was a man in a suit, looking back at her with a warm smile.

"It's not like it's stress. The interviewers said you were like this in the first and second interviews."

They were in an office.

Walls and ceiling painted white, not a speck of dust on the floor. Yoshino Nara sat in the center of the room on a folding chair, wearing a school unform.

But this was not the Isuzunomiya High uniform, for the simple reason that she was twelve years old and had just entered junior high. It was a good three years before she would meet Tougetsu Umidori.

"Sorry if it seems like a strange question, but I am in charge of this agency. I want to know as much about our talent as I can."

"......Hmm."

"No need to overthink it. I'll add that this will not be a factor in our decision to give you a contract."

The man in the suit—the president of this agency—glanced down at the paperwork on his desk.

"Yoshino Nara, applying for the model course, first-year student at a public junior high. You're the best-looking applicant in this round of auditions, hands down. I knew you'd received high evaluations from the staff administering the earlier interviews, but seeing your face with my own two eyes took my breath away."

He looked up, beheld her face again, and let out a sigh.

"You are very, very, very, very beautiful. I've been in this business a long time, and I've worked with all kinds of beautiful girls, yet I've never seen anyone as perfect as you, without a single flaw. I can't imagine any talent agencies would turn down a contract with you."

"Thank you."

"But that's why I'm asking. Yoshino Nara, why is it you're sitting through talent agency interviews with that sullen look on your face? That's one thing during your free time, but if you keep this up on the job, it can only lead to problems."

"No, I'll have no expression even on the job," Nara said.

"......What?"

"If I must give an answer to this, I will—the reason I have no expression is because I do not need one."

"......Huh?"

"Like you said yourself, my face is flawless. Perfect."

Nara nodded at that.

"I entirely agree. And for that reason, I cannot allow myself to make an expression. After all, my face is already perfect, flawless, complete. Adding anything unnecessary to it will only diminish that perfection. It will no longer be flawless. I show no emotions because doing so would only tarnish my beauty."

"............"

The president was left speechless for several seconds.

"......What are you talking about? Girls are cutest when they smile!"

"That may be true for other girls." Nara nodded. "But I'm different. Putting a smile on my face will not make me any cuter than I am now. I am already as cute as it is possible for me to be."

"..............."

Her utter confidence made him unsure how to argue the point. His brow twitched.

"W-well, a certain degree of eccentricity can be part of your charm. Let's try another question. Why do you want to be a model?"

"Because I have a pretty face," Nara said immediately. "Children who are good at sports try to become athletes. Kids who can draw try to become manga artists. The same logic applies here. I thought my natural beauty would come in handy."

"Uh-huh. That's a pretty normal motive, then."

He sounded relieved.

"Mm, I'm totally on board with that. Not everyone can make money from what they're good at."

"Money? I don't care about that."

"......You don't? Are you more into appearing in famous fashion shows?"

"Not really. Naturally, I realize that is an effective means of fulfilling my mission."

"……Mission?"

"Yes, my mission." Nara nodded, emphatic. "I must share my beauty with the world."

After that interview, Yoshino Nara did wind up joining the talent agency…but ultimately, the president's decision to hire her proved a grave mistake.

He really should have cut her loose right there.

No matter how good-looking she was, her behavior in the interview should have convinced him there was something wrong with her.

Had he realized this in time, he could have presented the unprecedented losses Yoshino Nara would cause.

It was all her fault.

"Explain yourself, Nara…!"

Three years since her interview.

His voice echoed through the office, laden with fury.

"Was this your plan all along…?"

There was no trace of the warm smile he'd worn at the interview. He was glaring fiercely at her, barely keeping his anger in check.

However, Nara herself didn't bat an eye. Her face never moved a muscle. She appeared to be simply staring into thin air.

"I don't know what you mean. I explained my position clearly during the interview."

"……Do you even understand what you've done? How much damage you've caused our agency?"

His voice was a hiss. He pulled several pages from a drawer and slammed them down on his desk.

"Sixteen! Sixteen promising talents, completely ruined! All because of you!"

The scattered pages all showed a headshot with a basic profile. The talent's résumés, sixteen in total. Mostly young women—but a few were male.

But the headshots were disturbing.

Each résumé listed a different name, date of birth—none of the profiles matched. But the headshots alone appeared to be identical.

Strictly speaking, they were not.

But all sixteen photos were of Yoshino Nara's face.

Not just the women—the men, too.

"No warning at all, completely out of the blue! Each one of them just showed up for work after getting plastic surgery to look like you!"

He twisted his face like he'd swallowed a bitter pill.

"By the time we noticed, it was too late. We asked why, and the victims all said the same thing. 'I wanted to be prettier. I wanted Yoshino Nara's face.'"

".............."

"I'll ask again, Nara. Was this your goal?"

"......Tell me, President," Nara said, her voice soft. "Have you ever heard of noblesse oblige?"

"......Huh?"

"The duty of the privileged. Those who are superior to others are obligated to use their talents and skills for the benefit of society. Someone like me was given a mission from God at the moment of my birth, and I cannot abandon it.

"President, what is my mission as the most beautiful girl alive?"

"......What are you talking about?"

"There's no use being indirect here. Let me state the facts as clearly as possible." Nara took a breath. "My birth was a message from God. The human race has no need of these futile discrepancies in our appearance. People should be valued for their insides alone, yet society evaluates them on the outsides they were born with—and this is a fatal flaw.

"I believe this was God's train of thought. Humanity is trapped in this never-ending spiral, and He wished to free us from it. But how? As long as people's faces are different, discrimination is inevitable. No matter how much we argue this should not be, humanity will continue to perceive value in the faces we are born with and never be free.

"In that case, the only option is to make us all look the same."

".................What?"

"That is why I was born, President. To unify the faces of humankind. I am the *model*, which all humankind will use to modify their features."

"......???"

"I'm confident that was God's goal. First, He caused the birth of someone with a flawless face, who could not possibly be cuter. Then He had me live an ordinary life. In doing so, He forced the people around me to take notice of my beauty.

"And those humans would reach the natural conclusion: 'Oh, how beautiful! In comparison, my own face is nothing! How ashamed I am. I envy the world's most beautiful person beyond measure! If only I could obtain that beauty myself!'

"——'Oh, but I can! I need merely get plastic surgery to look like her! Let's make an appointment today!'"

Nara reached the end of her speech and let out a sigh, leaning back.

"In other words, I was born the world's greatest beauty purely to plant that idea in the heads of those around me. That is the mission I was given. Still, making all of humanity voluntarily get plastic surgery? God has certainly given me a demanding task. Don't you agree?"

".........Um, have you lost it?"

The president's response was totally unfiltered.

"People the world over will admire you and choose plastic surgery? You mean that? That's ridiculous!"

"Naturally, I am aware. My mission is not something easily achieved." Nara shook her head.

"I chose to join the modeling world because I believed that was the most effective way to realize my mission. By modeling, I could spread my beauty to the world—I believed everyone who saw my photos would want to be like me and get plastic surgery accordingly."

"......Did you seriously think something that stupid would actually happen?"

"It *has* happened. If only to sixteen people over three whole years."

Her face blank, Nara let out a sigh.

"I imagine these sixteen already looked far better than the average human and were far more particular about their looks—and for that reason, they were far more impacted by their inferiority to my own."

"A-and you don't feel bad about that at all? It's your fault they've forever lost the faces their parents gave them!"

"Why should I care about that? Let me be clear, President, this has taken its toll on me, too," Nara growled. "When I decided to audition at this agency, I never imagined my plans would go this awry. I worked myself to the bone for three years and only managed to get sixteen people to improve themselves? What a disaster. I imagined that, by this stage, ninety percent of Japan would have fixed their faces."

"——I've heard enough! If I listen to you any longer, it'll drive *me* around the bend!"

The president was straight up shouting, trying to drown out Nara's drivel.

"You're fired, Yoshino Nara! Landing almost no gigs was bad enough, but I refuse to keep someone around who's actively destroying the rest of our roster! If you want to pull off this psychotic mission, go somewhere else!"

"......Yes, I planned to do just that," Nara said, her voice tamping down her own fury. "Continuing to work here will never allow me to achieve my goals. I had no intention of renewing my contract with you. We are done."

◇◇◇◇

"——In hindsight, that was childish of me," Nara admitted. "I'd been well aware that the agency staff would never appreciate my personal motives. Even if they asked directly, there was little point in explaining anything that would just make them deem me batshit crazy. Today, I would answer evasively, obscuring the point."

She was speaking reflectively, rambling on and on about her past— but Umidori was hardly in any state to pay attention.

"......?! ......?!"

Her mind was entirely on the mirror.

Reflected in it was her own face—now identical to Yoshino Nara's. It did not feel real at all. She kept prodding it with her fingers, yet it still didn't feel like her own flesh and blood. If her hair had not still been long and black, she might well never have realized this was meant to be her reflection.

"How does having my face feel, Umidori?" Nara asked, no tension in her tone whatsoever. "Do you like it? I'm quite confident you look good."

"......Wh-what? Why? What's going on?"

Umidori's mind could not process this. Could not accept what had happened to her. The one thing she knew was that Nara had put a hand to her face, the pain had been horrible, and then her features had wound up like this.

"Why would you do this, Nara?" Bullshit-chan hissed, one eye on Umidori's transformation.

——All three girls were sitting around the table again. Nara bolt upright. Umidori clutching the mirror, peering into it. And Bullshit-chan, grocery bags on the table in front of her, glaring across them at Nara.

"I'm completely failing to discern your intentions here."

"I don't get why not—I literally just explained them, Bullshit-chan. Ever since I was a child, I've dreamed of making all humankind get plastic surgery to look like me. Distribute my features to young and old, male and female, without discrimination. Remove the very concept of distinctive appearances from this world. To achieve this dream, to turn my desire to reality, I became a Beliar—apparently."

Like it was no concern of hers.

Nara turned back to Umidori.

"But I didn't really believe this goal could be achieved. I feel like I'm dreaming! Like this isn't actually real."

"......! Wh-what are you talking about, Nara?!" Umidori's voice was strangled, unnerved. "You want everyone to look exactly like you? That—that doesn't even make sense! And that's your heart's desire?!"

"Yes, indeed, Umidori. From the bottom of my heart, that is what I wish for. When I said I had no idea what this lie could be—I was fibbing.

"It's true that I didn't know the first thing about the Belied until I heard Bullshit-chan talking about them. But the moment she spelled it out, I knew I was a Beliar and that only this could be the lie I was attempting to falsify. I wasn't about to let you two murder this lie, so I started babbling to try to stave you off."

"......W-wait, Nara! This isn't right... I mean, you've never once said a word about anything like this......!"

"No, I didn't mention it. You didn't ask."

Nara shrugged.

"Likewise, I didn't know you were stealing pencils and eating them. All this time, it went right under my nose. That's how things go,

Umidori. I didn't know about your big secret, and you were clueless about mine. Nothing strange about that."

"..............!"

This was a forcible reminder of what Bullshit-chan's message had said.

Why? Because she's a Beliar.

She's fucked in the head.

She's a major threat.

...How well do you really know Nara?

"......That's not what I'm asking, Nara," Bullshit-chan said after a long silence. "I'm asking why you went to the trouble of confessing all this."

"............."

"Nara, do you even comprehend what you just did here?" Bullshit-chan asked, eyes on Nara, her voice soft. "You told us the lie you're telling. You spelled out in so many words exactly what you want falsified. That's tantamount to exposing your weakness. It's basically suicide."

And that really didn't seem to sit well with her.

"Honestly, I was careless. I left the two of you alone together, figuring that with your enemy offstage, you'd do something against Umidori. I just never imagined it would be so unhinged, so heedless of the consequences. Maybe I'm just making excuses, but if I'd known that—I'd have stuck to you like glue."

"......Hmph. Suicide?" Nara said, snorting, poker-faced. "I suppose you have a point. If I wish to protect my lie, then admitting to it is the last thing I should do. And I did actually start by insisting I had no clue what my lie was, fully intent on playing dumb until your life ran out, Bullshit-chan. And yet I turned around and blabbed all the details of my lie. Perhaps you're right—perhaps I am suicidal."

"......Stop beating around the bush, Nara. I'm asking *why* you did that."

"Because I didn't want to kill you."

"..............Huh?" Bullshit-chan was clearly floored by that. "...... What?"

"It's pretty straightforward, Bullshit-chan. I meant to keep quiet until your life ran out... But then I realized you'd be dead, and I decided to change my tactics.

"Bullshit-chan, perhaps we are enemies, locked in a battle only one of us can survive. But is that really the only option available to us? Is there truly no way to avert your death without killing my lie?"

".............What are you talking about?"

"For example, what about this? You decide not to pursue this fallicide and go after a different target."

".......A different target?"

"You've still got a whole week left. If our skill for sniffing out lies works like human noses, it shouldn't be impossible. And when you find them, the three of us can team up to help you devour that lie."

".........Huh?!"

"I think it's a pretty good idea. And I'd argue that teaming up to kill a different lie has greater odds of succeeding than the two of you trying to kill my lie."

"..............."

Bullshit-chan stared back at her, stunned. "I—I don't know what you mean. Where's this all coming from, Nara? I mean, I get the logic of it, but...but that would only help me. There's nothing in it for you."

"No, that's not true, Bullshit-chan," Nara said. "I mean, if you don't die, then Tougetsu Umidori will eventually be capable of lying."

".............Huh?"

Umidori's head snapped up.

She'd had her eyes locked on the mirror the whole time they'd been talking, but Nara's last statement finally pulled her out of that.

"That's why I've spilled the beans, Bullshit-chan. I want to help you. I don't want to let you die if you there's a chance you can save Umidori."

Nara turned to her friend.

"Umidori, you don't want Bullshit-chan dying, do you?"

"............."

Umidori didn't immediately manage a response.

"Wh-why......?" she croaked after a long pause. Her voice rather feeble.

"Huh? Why? I mean, I heard everything you talked about through the toilet door. That includes the reward Bullshit-chan offered for assisting with her fallicide. Umidori, you only agreed to help her so you can learn to lie!

"Honestly, that's not something I can ever help you with. The only thing I can do is plaster my face on other people. Seeking out a Beliar who can cure Umidori is a task only a living lie with a decade of experience can manage. Only Bullshit-chan can do that for you."

"......N-no, I don't mean that," Umidori said, shaking her head. "Wh-why are you worried about what would happen to me if Bullshit-chan died, Nara? Whether I can lie doesn't affect you one way or the other."

"......Huh?" Nara made a noise that sounded utterly baffled. "I don't get why you're asking. Isn't it obvious? Because I like you."

"Oh?"

"Is any other reason necessary? Like I said while we were hugging: I'm on your side." Nara shrugged. "If someone you like's in trouble, there's nothing strange about trying to help them out."

".........Nara," Umidori said, at a loss for words.

Nara's face didn't move.

The two girls sat perfectly still, staring at each other.

——Meanwhile, Bullshit-chan was studying Nara's face, her hackles raised.

"I can't believe what I'm hearing. Do you mean that, Nara? You just want to help Umidori? No other tricks or schemes? For that alone, you revealed yourself and are attempting to negotiate peace?"

"Yes, that's exactly it, Bullshit-chan. If I don't admit I'm a Beliar who's well aware of my own lie, we can't even begin to negotiate.

"Changing Umidori's face is part of that. I could explain my lie all day, but a demonstration makes it easier for you both to fully understand it."

"......And you don't mind if your lie ends up getting killed because of this reckless decision?" Bullshit-chan asked, feeling it out.

"......No, that's an entirely separate matter," Nara said, shaking her head. "I'm still hell-bent on protecting my lie. Just...in my mind, that decision doesn't contradict the desire to help you two."

"..............."

"Well, what do you say? Can we make peace? Or not?"

".........A-absolutely not!" Bullshit-chan snapped, her voice rising. "Like you said yourself, we're mortal enemies! Only one of us can survive this! There's no path to peace after all this!"

"......Why not? There's no real reason for us to be at each other's throats. I simply want to save my lie, and as long as some other lie fills your belly, isn't that—?"

"No, that's not true. It *has* to be *your* lie."

"............Huh?"

"Whether I live or die *no longer matters*," Bullshit-chan said. She turned toward Umidori—eyes on the face Nara had transformed. "You want to change the face of everyone on earth to match your own. Mm-hmm. As long as you're possessed of an idea that dangerous, I cannot let you be. We have to murder your lie right here and now. Should we fail, Nara, you will become an enemy of the world. A societal evil. Just like *them*."

She was spitting words, sounding absolutely furious.

Nara crooked her head.

"......? I have no clue what you're talking about. An enemy of the world? Societal evil? Who is *them*?"

"......Um," Bullshit-chan said. But before she could speak further—

——*Ding-dong.*

The sound of the doorbell echoed through the room.

5

A Painful Defeat

Would she live or die today?

Would she eat or be eaten?

Unable to rely on anyone, no solace anywhere, getting through it on her own.

She was like a stray cat, abandoned by her Beliar; that was Bullshit-chan's lot, her daily grind.

"Hahh, hahh, hahh......!"

A year before Bullshit-chan visited Tougetsu Umidori's home.

On a street in a city in a prefecture...somewhere.

Covered in wounds, Bullshit-chan stumbled down an alley behind an arcade at night.

"Wh-whew... Just barely pulled off that fallicide."

Unsteady on her feet, badly out of breath, the words tumbled out.

"Honestly, I really thought I was a goner. If that Beliar hadn't let go of their desire at a critical juncture, I'd no longer exist."

It was hard to tell in this darkness, but her cat-ear hoodie was torn up, and fresh blood was oozing out from the cuts.

Bullshit-chan was a lie and functionally immortal; no matter how much damage her flesh took, she should be able to recover it instantly. But this time, she'd been roughed up so bad her healing couldn't keep up.

"A-at any rate, I've bought myself a few more months of life. Ah-ha-ha-ha-ha... By the skin of my teeth."

As she muttered to herself, a look of infinite relief crossed her face. But it soon faded.

"......Ha-ha, I pulled through and survived today, but to what end?" she asked herself, her tone souring. "Day after day after day, I have nothing on my mind but turning other lies into food. Ten years clinging to life for no better reason than 'I don't want to die.' How wretched is that? Even I'm appalled by this squalid struggle. Heh-heh..."

As she grumbled, she staggered on—until her legs buckled under her, and she toppled over, slamming hard into the alley wall.

"Ow!"

With an undignified grunt, she slid right down to the ground.

"......Ugh, worst night ever," Bullshit-chan groaned, flat on her face. "I guess this hoodie's done for. Gotta go buy a new one..."

——Naturally, in this back alley, there were no humans to come running, help her up, to fuss over her.

A few dozen yards off, there were crowds thronging. The lights of the main street gleaming.

It was all so very close, yet this dimly lit alley might as well have been another world. One devoid of warmth.

"............"

Bullshit-chan lay still, gazing absently at those glittering lights.

"If I was a human girl, perhaps I could have gone to school."

An idle thought that no one else could hear.

——Or so she assumed.

"Oh? Aren't you a curious one."

The voice echoed from directly above.

"You want to attend human school? You're the first lie I've seen who seemed anything *like* this human."

"......Huh?"

A man stood over her.

Tall, black hair, late thirties.

Hands in his pockets, a smile plastered on his face, staring down at her.

"You really are the most irregular lie, Bullshit-chan," he said. "Most lies are done for the moment their host abandons them. To think you could extend your life in such an unorthodox manner, patching yourself up with other lies. And to keep that up for a full decade—that is hardly a sane act. Tenacious to a downright astonishing degree."

The man's most visually distinctive feature would be his hat.

It was badly fitted and filthy. A mud-colored hat that blended into the night, depressing to even look at.

"Wh-what the hell are you? Who are you? How do you know my name......?"

Unable to pick herself up but suitably taken aback, Bullshit-chan could only lie there asking questions.

The man in the hat offered no clear answers, merely a message.

"Bullshit-chan, would you care to join us?"

"......Huh?"

"If you become one of us, you'll never have to worry about your next meal."

"....................What?"

——That was how Bullshit-chan first met *them*.

◇◇◇◇

The sound of the doorbell echoed through the room. Their conversation died.

Nara turned her masklike face toward the door.

"What? A visitor? At this hour?" she grumbled. "This is an important conversation! Umidori, do you have any clue who this is?"

"......N-no, not at all," Umidori said, shaking her head. "I really don't talk to any neighbors. Maybe they've got the wrong room?"

——*Ding-dong. Ding-dong. Ding-dong.*

But her words were soon denied. They kept ringing.

"Umidori, are you sure you've been paying your rent?" Nara asked.

"I've never missed a payment!" Umidori wailed, but even as she denied it: "...........?"

She caught sight of Bullshit-chan's demeanor, and the words died on her lips.

——All color had drained from the girl's face. Her head was down, and she was visibly shaken.

"......Bullshit-chan?"

"..........No way," she squeaked. "Showing up right as I'm about to talk about them? That's just uncanny!"

"..............?"

——*Ding-dong. Ding-dong. Ding-dong. Ding-dong.*

Again, the doorbell echoed, so many times they could no longer count how many.

"......Uh, Umidori, at least look through the peephole?" Nara said, clearly on guard.

Umidori nodded. "Uh, yeah, I'll do that. You two wait here."

She got up to move away——

——*Wham!*

With a loud noise, the door to Umidori's apartment was blown away.

"——Hah?" Umidori gasped.

No longer attached to its hinges, the metal door flew right past her. The massive chunk of iron hit the living room wall with a heavy thud, cracking the plaster.

"..............Huuuh?!"

The remains of the door hit the floor, bounced a few times, and then lay still. Umidori was still just making dazed noises.

"Is your doorbell broken?"

A moment later, a young woman's voice—one Umidori had never heard before—came from the entrance.

"..............?!"

Umidori turned toward her on reflex, and the shocking sight kept her speechless.

In the ruined doorway stood a strange woman with bandages wound around her eyes.

"Did you not hear me ringing the bell? Repeatedly? There was no response at all, so I was forced to kick down the door."

Purple hair.

She wore a thin nightgown, like something you'd wear at a hospital.

She was slightly shorter than Umidori.

Standing there in the apartment hall, not even bothering to take off her shoes.

"............Wh-who are you?!" Umidori managed after a moment of silence.

——What was with this lady?

"Ah-ha. I see what's going on here."

As if she hadn't heard Umidori's question, the mystery lady swiveled her head—despite the bandages entirely blocking her eyesight—to survey the room.

"No wonder you were so easy to find. This place reeks of falsehood. Someone in this room must be a Beliar."

"......Huh?"

"Perhaps *must* is the wrong word. If the odor is this powerful, it's a dead cert."

Heels clicking, the bandage lady stalked over to the table.

"*You're* the Beliar. I'm right, aren't I?" she said, standing right in front of Yoshino Nara.

".................Um," Nara said, gazing up at her—her voice as vacant as her expression.

Clearly, she was as dumbfounded by this intruder as Umidori.

"Hmph, it's not every day we come across a lie with a stench this overwhelming. Wonderful. I just adore people like you! Do go on, spread your lies willy-nilly." The bandage lady gave her a satisfied nod, then said, "But I am not here to speak to *humans*."

She turned to face the white-haired girl in a cat-ear hoodie sitting directly between Umidori and Nara.

"It's been a while, kitty cat. How fare you?"

"Hurt..." Bullshit-chan forced a smile to her lips, staring up at the enigmatic intruder. "What brings you here?"

"Ha-ha, that's quite a greeting. After all I did for you. Are you not pleased to see a former comrade?"

The bandage lady—Hurt?—twisted her lips into a malevolent grin.

"You ungrateful wretch. I never imagined you'd vanish without so much as a by-your-leave. Oh, how I grieved. I'm so stricken I chased you all the way here."

"..............."

Bullshit-chan's cheek twitched, her eyes locked on Hurt with unprecedented intensity. Sweat was beading on her brow, but she made no attempt to wipe it.

"——Er, um, Hurt?"

Another young woman's voice came from the door.

"Should I come in, too?"

There stood a woman in her midtwenties, wearing a long skirt.

Brown hair, big round eyes. All spindly lines, giving her a delicate, fragile, wimpy vibe.

Her gaze darted anxiously around the room, never settling down.

Hurt didn't even bother turning toward her.

"——Hayakawa, you are an unfathomable drip. Can you not even make that judgment call without asking my opinion?" Really laying it on thick. "Have I *ever* given you permission to leave my side? Get in here this instant."

"......R-right."

Hayakawa scurried across the room—she *did* take off her shoes—moving to Hurt's side.

"Tch! Your sole gift in life is for aggravation. Will the day ever arrive when you manage to do something that doesn't get right up my left nostril?"

"I-I'm sorry, Hurt..."

"Lord, making someone like you my partner is the greatest blot upon my life."

"............"

——As they spoke, Umidori just gaped at them.

None of this made sense.

Who were these people?

Two total strangers, breaking down her door and forcing their way into her apartment?

"Don't worry, Umidori, Nara," Bullshit-chan said, sensing her consternation. "Hurt would never kill a civilian. As long as you both sit quietly, you will mostly likely probably maybe not be in any danger."

Her voice was calm, but her expression anything but.

"At the least, you two won't be..."

"...Ooh? You're still capable of giving advice, kitty cat? Or does that mean you're unaware of your own predicament?"

"............."

Bullshit-chan and Hurt glared at each other across the tiny table. The tense silence lasted several seconds.

"——Rahhhhhh!"

Bullshit-chan moved first.

With a roar, she grabbed the table by a leg, flinging it at Hurt—with the grocery bags on top.

".....Huh?!" Umidori gulped, shocked by this turn of events.

Hurt had been directly across from Bullshit-chan, so the table hit her head-on, and the sound of the impact echoed through the room. The contents of the grocery bags flew everywhere.

"——!"

Bullshit-chan was already on her feet, trying to slip past Hurt and flee the room. A few steps later...

"——Augh?!"

...she let out a little scream and drew up short, crumpling to the floor.

——No, perhaps it was more accurate to say she became physically incapable of running any longer. Why? Because both her ankles had been severed cleanly, as if sliced by piano wire.

".....................?! N-noooooooooooo!" Umidori shrieked. She clapped both hands over her mouth, eyes locked on the *stumps*. "B-Bullshit-chan?! Wh-why...? How?!"

"O-oww......!"

Blub, blub—blood spurted out of her ankles. She was groaning aloud.

"Ow, ow, ow, ow, owww...!"

"You fool. I'd never let you run," Hurt growled, looming over her. That table had hit her head-on, but she'd suffered zero injuries.

"No, you weren't trying to run—you were attempting to put distance between yourself and those girls? Whatever, just stay docile if you wish to avoid undue suffering."

Even as she spoke, Hurt mercilessly stomped on Bullshit-chan's legs, despite the girl showing no signs of further resistance.

"Gahhh?!"

Bullshit-chan let out a wheezing groan, like a bug getting squished.

"——! H-hey, stop that! What's the idea?!" Umidori cried, unable to beat it. "Wh-who the hell are you?! Bursting in here, doing horrible things to Bullshit-chan......! Get away from her th-this instant!"

She clearly did not have the first clue what was going on here, but seeing Bullshit-chan in pain made her start to get up—

"Shush."

"......Huh?"

"Do not speak, human. This is none of your business."

Hurt's voice was flat. She didn't even glance at Umidori.

"Or do you wish to lose your feet like this kitty cat has?"

——Her flat tones took on a level of chilling hostility no ordinary mortal could ever muster.

"Eek?!"

It hit Umidori like a truck, and she let out a pathetic squeak, her butt hitting the floor.

"......?! ......?!"

That was all it took to leave her flapping her mouth like a fish, unable to make a single sound. Her whole body flinched so hard she could barely draw breath.

——Wh-who was this lady? How was she so terrifying?!

"Now then, is your mind made up, kitty cat?"

With Umidori silenced, Hurt appeared to forget she even existed. Her attention was fully on Bullshit-chan.

"Let me remind you—you did this to yourself, traitor. Did you think you'd be safe if you simply fled to the west side of Japan? Hardly. You could run to the other side of the earth, and I would still hunt you down."

"......! Why?!" Bullshit-chan managed, squeezing her words out between ragged gasps for air despite the foot grinding against her legs. "H-he'd never order something like this! That man—Mud Hat would never interfere with what I'm doing! That's why I didn't think anyone would come after me so soon after I ran. So why...?!"

"Hmph, you're right there, kitty cat. He knows you've betrayed us, but he did not order your pursuit."

Hurt snorted, clearly resenting this fact.

"This is entirely *my* decision. He issues no orders. I have come to finish you off of my own free will. For the simple reason that I *despise* you."

"...............!"

"I saw a perfect opportunity to put down a disgusting piece of vermin. Mud Hat made no attempt to stop me, either. He doesn't interfere."

"......I've been meaning to ask," Bullshit-chan said, looking up at Hurt. "Why *do* you have it in for me? What did I ever do to you?"

"——Hmph, a stupid question." Hurt smirked. "Your very existence galls me."

"......Does it?"

"You're a disgrace to all lies, kitty cat. I cannot stomach the fact that you've eked out a life for ten whole years."

Hurt spat her words, kicking one of the grocery bags for emphasis.

"Take this food. You were planning on *cooking* something with it, weren't you? You love to cook, which is patently absurd. A feeble imitation of humankind. We're lies—we don't *need* food!

"You're a sham human, kitty cat. And worse—you fear death just like they do. A disgrace to all lies! I can't abide your very way of life. If you insist on embarrassing us further, then I'll personally finish you off right here."

Hurt spat all that in a single breath, then stomped on Bullshit-chan again.

"...............〰〰〰〰〰!" The pain proved so great that her scream did not even make a sound.

"That's enough."

——Just then, a firm voice echoed through the room.

"You burst in here and made a scene—who are you?"

Yoshino Nara.

She was up on her feet, glaring at Hurt, without moving a muscle on her face.

"Move away from Bullshit-chan."

A few seconds of silence. "What?" Hurt said, turning toward her and looking surprised.

"I don't know who you are or what's between you and Bullshit-chan, but she and I were in the middle of an important conversation. If you've got business with her, at least have the courtesy to wait until we're through."

"......Now I'm the one lost here. What does this kitty cat have to do with you? What were you up to before I came in?"

"Well—"

"No, don't tell me. I can imagine. This kitty cat tried to eat your lie, yes? She's a bottom-feeder, unable to sustain herself without eating other falsehoods."

Hurt's lips twisted in a sneer.

"But you really are a magnificent Beliar, human. The smell coming off you is far more intense than your average Belied. It speaks to the strength of your desire. I'd be willing to introduce you to Mud Hat."

"......Hmm?"

"A Beliar like you would likely meet with his approval."

"......Mud Hat?" Her face never moved, but Nara sounded taken aback. "I don't even know who that is!"

"Pfft. The kitty cat hasn't told you yet? Not a word about that man— the liefluencer?"

"......??"

"Just hold your horses. Before anything else, I need to put this kitty cat down."

As she spoke, Hurt turned back toward Bullshit-chan.

"You stand there quietly, watching me finish her off. Once that's done, I'd be willing to personally introduce you to Mud Hat. Don't worry, this will all be over in an instant."

"......Huh?! No, I said stop!"

When Hurt tried to force the conversation to a close, Nara angrily grabbed her shoulder.

"We're not done here!"

"......Who do you think you are?" Hurt growled, not even turning to her. "Why are you trying to save the kitty cat? You're a Beliar. She's your mortal enemy!"

"——Hmph, like I care!" Nara snapped. "Logic has no place here. I hate to repeat myself, but Bullshit-chan and I were having an important conversation. Then your wack ass barged in, interrupted us, and started torturing her? I'm not just gonna stand here twiddling my thumbs!"

"............"

For a long moment, Hurt fell silent.

"Ah," she said at length. "I see you need to suffer some consequences."

She brushed Nara's hand off her shoulder.

"Brace yourself, human. You're about to find out who the superior species is," she growled, swinging around to face Nara and grabbing a handful of her shirt. "I won't *kill* you—I'll leave you clinging to life, in enough pain you'll never dare talk back to me again. A lifetime of agony is a small price to pay for annoying *me*."

"............" Even with this lady making threats to her face, Nara didn't bat an eye.

And in that moment—

——there was a spurting sound. Fresh blood spraying.

"......Wh...at?"

A voice, raised in disbelief.

But it didn't belong to Yoshino Nara.

"How...is this......?" Hurt gasped, gazing at the scalpel-like blades stabbing her all over. She coughed, puking up blood...and crumpled to the ground.

"——Know your place, shit for brains."

A young woman's voice, echoing from somewhere, belonging to no one present.

"Laying a finger on my Yoshino is the height of arrogance. You should be eternally grateful your punishment was only full-body slices."

Not from *somewhere*.

That voice was echoing from *within Nara's body*.

"......Oh, I get it," Nara said, nodding to herself. "I suppose she did establish this point—that line about the scent of a powerful lie coming from my body. In other words, you've been inside me this whole time."

She was talking to this mystery voice as if it were an old friend.

"I imagine I've made things rather difficult for you. Getting stuck inside me, unable to take a single step outside—that must have been stifling."

"——Mm, heh-heh-heh. Yoshino, no need to offer consolation. I'm very comfortable inside you. Not once have I ever felt confined."

"Oh? Well, I'm glad to hear that. But I suppose it's high time I released you. Come out, and show yourself to your master."

"——Gladly."

And true to its word—

—something rather like a human body sprouted from Nara's back, falling free of her and stepping down onto the floor.

A naked woman.

She stood bolt upright, her back perfectly straight. She appeared to be no older than Nara. Long arms and legs, an hourglass figure, and pale pink hair like the Yoshino cherry.

But the most striking thing about her was her face—which was indistinguishable from Yoshino Nara's own.

"Hmm. So that's what you look like," Nara said, clearly impressed. Her eyes exploring the nude doppelganger's figure. "It's the strangest feeling. I only just became aware of your existence, and yet this doesn't feel like our first encounter. It's like we've been together as long as I can remember. I wonder why that is?"

"Simple. I've *always* been here inside you, Yoshino." The stark-naked schoolgirl smiled. "I've been possessing you since the moment you first told a lie. We are of the same mind and body. I'm so glad we finally get a chance to speak like this.

"Call me Envy Sakura, Yoshino. Envy Sakura is my name. Born purely to make your wish come true, your dedicated partner. A pleasure to meet you."

"——Wh-what's your problem?!" Hurt snarled from the floor at her feet.

She was covered in blood, lying prostate. Her wounds would have killed a human—and clearly, they were no trifle to a lie, either.

"You're the lie possessing her? You think you have a right to do this to—"

"Shut your foul mouth, butterface."

Even as Hurt gasped out the words, the naked girl—Envy Sakura— spun around and stomped her.

"Gah?!"

"You're the one who attacked Yoshino. A minor threat like that cat rolling around over there is one thing, but I'm hardly optimistic enough to sit back and watch while a creature like you mishandles my host.

"How dare you even dream of harming my Yoshino! That sin demands a thousand deaths!"

As she spoke, Envy Sakura held out her palm toward Hurt; a moment later, a torrent of blades flew out of it, raining down on the lie below.

"Gahhhhhhhhhh?!"

The scream sounded like a death rattle. It filled the very room. Hurt had been badly torn up to begin with, and these new cuts dug so deep she lost her very shape. No longer physically capable of moving at all, she could only scream.

"Wahhhh..."

This panicked noise came from the girl in the long skirt, Hayakawa. She'd been lurking to one side this whole time.

"H-Hurt... Wh-what do I do? I don't—"

"Mm, well done, Envy Sakura. I think that should suffice," Nara said.

And with that praise, she spun around.

"I say we beat a retreat for now," she said, addressing Umidori—who was still flat on her ass.

"......Huh?"

"Don't just sit there, Umidori. Surely, you've figured it out by now? The bandage lady lying there—" Nara jerked a thumb toward Hurt. "She kicked in a steel door and sliced off Bullshit-chan's ankles— she's clearly not human! It's safe to assume she's a manifest lie, like Bullshit-chan.

"And if she's also immortal, then she'll easily recover from these injuries. In which case, we'd better run for it. Get somewhere she won't catch up with us—*now*."

"..............!"

That certainly brought Umidori back to her senses.

This series of dizzying twists had left her brain scrambled, but Nara's clear directive helped her refocus. Yes, they had to get out of here. She didn't want to spend another second in this freakspace; they could hash out the details once they were safely away.

And with that decided, Umidori knew what to do.

"B-Bullshit-chan...!" she yelled, running over to the girl lying immobile on the floor.

"Unhh......!"

Bullshit-chan was flat on her face, badly weakened but still technically conscious. Umidori scooped her frail frame into her arms.

"——I gotcha!" she said, putting her on her back. "Y-you okay, Bullshit-chan? I mean, I can see you aren't, but......!"

"......n't."

"Huh?"

"......................I can't."

A feeble whisper in her ear. The cry of a girl at the end of her rope.

"*Sniff.* Unhhhhhhh... I can't do this anymore... No more pain, no more fear..."

"......B-Bullshit-chan?"

Alarmed, Umidori looked back.

And found the girl on her back shaking like a leaf, huge tears flowing down her cheeks.

"Wahhhhhhhhhhhhh! Wahhhhhhhhhhhhhhhh!"

"................"

In all their interactions, Bullshit-chan had never betrayed a sign of such fragility—and it hit Umidori hard.

No signs of her default aplomb, she'd been reduced to a sniveling mess. Had this attack been that traumatic? Certainly, anyone would be messed up if they lost their ankles.

"......! Nara, I've got Bullshit-chan! I'm ready when you are!"

Concluding she could think about this later, Umidori tore her mind away, calling out to her friend.

"Okay. Thanks, Umidori. Let's get out of this place. Envy Sakura, I assume you're coming?"

"But of course, Yoshino." She alone had been standing there, above the fray—but she nodded at Nara's call. "Just give me three more seconds."

With that, she moved away from the entrance, striding toward the curtain-covered window.

——And without a moment's hesitation, she ripped it to pieces.

"......Huh?!"

That was the last thing Umidori expected; she forgot everything else and froze on the spot.

Hands moving quickly, Envy Sakura draped the shredded curtain around her body like a dress. In mere seconds, her voluptuous body was covered by that thin cloth.

"Thanks for waiting, Yoshino. We're good to go."

"..............."

Envy Sakura struck a smug pose, wearing the remains of Umidori's curtain.

This certainly rattled Umidori, but clearly this was not the time to be concerned about her apartment's accoutrements. The sacrifice of a curtain or two was well worth the price of a clean getaway.

"Th-then let's run for it!" she yelled, and all of them headed for the door.

"......! Y-you bastards! You'll pay for this!"

Hurt was screaming threats at their fleeing backs, but none of them turned to look.

6

Mud Hat

Outside the apartment building, they ran all the way to the nearest train station.

It was eight thirty. There were still suits heading home from work and students returning from after-school activities; the crowd was hardly thin.

"I-I'm down with running, but any idea where, Nara?!"

Despite the crowds, Umidori was almost shrieking.

She was still carrying Bullshit-chan, but she was darting her eyes constantly, scanning their surroundings.

"A train? Or a taxi? Where to?! Should we abandon this prefecture entirely?!"

"Calm yourself, Umidori," Nara said, as collected as her friend wasn't. "I'm not exactly sure how long it'll take that Hurt character to heal her wounds and come after us, but she was pretty badly messed up. At the very least, she won't be hot on our heels. There's no need for excessive alarm. In fact, this is our best chance to settle down and think clearly. We should take advantage of it."

"D-do we have that kind of leeway, Nara?! I don't know what that woman is, but she's bad news! No telling how bad things will go the next time she catches up! We've gotta get to safety ASAP!"

"Yes, Umidori. She was a dangerous opponent. On that I agree." Nara sighed, nodding. "But one other thing is true. *'Run as far as we can go!'*

'*Hide somewhere she'll never find us.*' Those options are *not* on the table right now.

"After all, our enemy is a lie—like Bullshit-chan, she can *smell* us out. As long as you are with a Beliar like me and a manifest lie like Bullshit-chan, she's basically got a high-spec GPS tracking attached to us. Escape is no more an option than lying low. No matter what we do, she *will* find us, and she *will* catch up."

"......Th-that's worse! Then there's nothing we can do!"

"I didn't say that. Right, Envy Sakura?" Nara turned to the lie next to her. "I imagine you know what I want you to do without me having to spell it out in words."

"Right you are, Yoshino." Envy Sakura nodded.

She was only wearing a curtain over her birthday suit, and it was downright provocative. Yet she was acting like a total boss, no trace of shame, moving confidently at Nara's side.

Identical faces. Pale pink hair to her hips. An ample chest. Long, slim legs.

Standing side by side, their faces matched, making them look like sisters.

"Me knowing what's on your mind is such a given I almost wish you hadn't asked," Envy Sakura said with a smug smirk. "In fact, I've already carried out the order you were about to give me."

"..............?"

Umidori blinked, not following their conversation. Still...

"——Huh?"

——She might have been a bit slow on the uptake, but it didn't take her long to pick up on the changes around them.

They were standing in the clearing outside the station. A dozen or so commuters were walking past them, heading home from the station gates. And the change was affecting everything above their neck.

Every face was identical.

And not just that.

Their faces were perfect, beautiful beyond compare—just like the girl standing next to Umidori.

"Behold, Umidori," Nara said, looking her in the eye. "Envy Sakura's powers have put my face on everyone in the vicinity."

".......Huh?!"

"Naturally, the world itself has not yet been affected. This is merely a localized phenomenon. I have only shared my beauty with the people of this neighborhood."

Nara spun around, basking in the sights.

"Take one step out of this area, and their faces will return to normal. But that works both ways; anyone coming in from the outside will soon bear my face."

".......?! W-wait a second, Nara! Why would you do that now?!"

"To provide cover, Umidori."

".......Cover?"

"Our enemy is tracking us via the smell of a lie. In which case, I need only permeate the entire town with that fragrance, rendering her nose useless. Less a blindfold than a nose plug. Even then, my scent—and Bullshit-chan's—will be far stronger than anyone around us, so assume this is merely a stalling tactic."

"..............."

Even as she listened to Nara's explanation, Umidori was gazing at the scene in shock.

Two junior high girls were moving past her. "Like, did your face just hurt for no reason? What was that about?" "I know, right? It was over quick, but I could barely stand up!" "At least it's over now, I guess."

It didn't seem like anyone affected even realized their faces had changed. The lie had falsified the world, rewritten common knowledge. The girls themselves no longer remembered their original faces. If what Nara said was true, this only affected their vicinity—but imagining this change transforming the entire world sent a chill down Umidori's spine.

"Well, this should eliminate the immediate threat," Nara said, sounding pleased with herself. "Let's find somewhere to collect ourselves."

◇◇◇◇

They retreated to a family restaurant.

This was Nara's idea. "Better to join the throngs than to try to isolate ourselves. I think the lie I've spread will provide better camouflage that way."

So far, she was right. It helped that the dinner rush was still going, and there were plenty of other diners in the restaurant. They were seated at the one empty booth in the back. It made sense, as it would likely take Hurt a while to find them here.

Still.

"*Sniff*. Wah...!"

Even at the table, Bullshit-chan was not yet capable of speech.

"Unh...unh...unhhhhhhh......!"

She was bawling her eyes out.

Her shoulders heaved as she sobbed, fountains of tears welling up from her eyes.

Both her ankles had already healed, but they hadn't thought to grab her shoes, so she'd been left barefoot. At the very least, she *appeared* to have no lasting injuries. Clearly, the damage she'd sustained was all internal—and not so easily healed.

"......Um, Bullshit-chan, seriously, are you okay?" Umidori asked, unable to bear it. She was sitting on Bullshit-chan's left. "Um, I could go get you something hot from the drink bar?"

"......! N-no, that won't be necessary, Umidori," Bullshit-chan said, dismissing her. "I-I'll stop crying in another forty—fifty seconds. And I promise...I will explain all that."

Even as she spoke, she started patting the area around her eyes with both palms. Stimulating her eyeballs to try to force the tear ducts closed?

"............"

But to Umidori, this was just proof that Bullshit-chan was not doing well. She automatically looked to Nara.

"......Yeah, she's in bad shape," Nara said, meeting her gaze and shrugging. "Fine! Umidori, you look after her awhile. Envy Sakura and I will go grab us some drinks."

"Uh, okay. Sure. Thanks, Nara."

Umidori nodded. Nara waved her hand like it was nothing and stood up.

"Yoshino, there's no reason why we should do anything for this cat," Envy Sakura said, clearly disgruntled. "She can fetch her own drinks. We may have wound up fleeing together, but she's not our friend."

"Now, now, don't be so hostile, Envy Sakura," Nara said, sighing.

"Come what may, our priority right now is getting her back on her feet. If you don't want to come, I'll go on my own."

"......! W-wait, Yoshino! I'm not about to let you be her errand girl!"

Nara's sulky tone had clearly gotten to Envy Sakura, and she hastily stood up. The two of them headed off to the drink bar.

"......Whew," Umidori said once they'd moved away.

She pulled a plain handkerchief from her skirt pocket.

"Bullshit-chan, sit still."

As Umidori spoke, she turned toward the other girl and began gently dabbing at her moistened eyes.

"......Eep?! Wh-what are you doing, Umidori?"

Bullshit-chan had not expected to have a cloth pressed over her eyes, and she freaked out a bit.

"S-stop that! I didn't ask you to...!"

"Ack, don't squirm. It's hard to clean up tears on your own, you know."

Bullshit-chan was flapping her arms around, trying to duck away from the handkerchief.

"......! S-seriously, I'll be fine, Umidori! All outward damage my body took is healed up! I'm just a bit of an emotional wreck because... well, that really rattled me."

"A bit, my foot. You're shaking like a kitten caught in the rain. White as a sheet."

"N-not true! I'm not a fragile lie! It takes a lot more than that to get me down! I-I've survived crises like this any number of times!"

"......It's really not convincing when I can hear the tears in your voice," Umidori said, half smiling, trying to soothe her. "Right now, you need to calm down. I know we don't have a lot of time, but Nara and I are not trying to rush you more than strictly necessary."

"............"

Bullshit-chan's tears were still flowing, but she shot Umidori a look of wordless protest.

"......If you have to wipe my tears, at least use those paper napkins over there."

"Huh?"

"Otherwise, my tears will stain your handkerchief."

"......So?" Umidori genuinely didn't seem to get what that meant.

"Wh-why's that a problem? I don't care about *that*. Bullshit-chan, your tears aren't *dirty*."

".......Everything about me is," Bullshit-chan whispered, slowly shaking her head. "Honestly, you're too good for this world, Umidori. I'm just a filthy stray cat, nothing in my head but where my next meal's coming from. I mean, sure, cats are cute, but I'm not even *that*—only a crazy person would be nice to me. Did you forget about the Pencil Thief thing?"

"Hmm?"

"It may have been a necessary step for my planned fallicide, but I revealed your biggest secret to Nara! She deep-fried your entire pencil collection! Aren't you at least a little mad at me?"

"............."

This just made Umidori's eyes dart about in confusion.

"I mean, it's not like I have no thoughts on that subject, but this is hardly the time or the place. And...Bullshit-chan, it's not like you did anything bad."

"......I didn't?"

"I mean, I stole and ate Nara's pencils. That's clearly wrong!" Umidori insisted, looking Bullshit-chan right in the eye. "All you did was drag that wrong out into the light of day. I'm not nearly asinine enough to try to blame you for that. And since it ultimately didn't harm my relationship with Nara, I don't even have a reason to hold it against you."

"............." Bullshit-chan was gaping at her. Genuinely shocked by her words. "......I guess this is what *too appalled to speak* means. You really are a pure soul, Umidori.

"Honestly, if you're that gullible, I'm scared for your future. Someone's gonna take you for a sucker and fleece you for all you're worth. To a bad girl like me, you've as good as got a target painted on you."

——But in marked contrast to her words, Bullshit-chan had latched on to Umidori's free hand.

"Mm?"

"......Don't read too much into it. This is the logical conclusion of my rational mind," Bullshit-chan insisted, not meeting Umidori's gaze and tightening her grip. "You're right. It doesn't feel like I can regain control of my emotions on my own. I'm hoping holding your hand will be an effective antidote.

"I heard somewhere that physical contact is the best way to soothe a storm inside. Don't underestimate touch. And if merely shaking your hand will let me calm down, then why would I not try it?"

"……Okay…," Umidori said, scratching her cheek. "……So basically, you're scared, so you wanna hold hands?"

"……! Absolutely not! Do not treat me like a baby! This is a practical solution to the immediate problem! Umidori, are you even following the conversation?"

Bullshit-chan unleashed a torrent of words, effectively silencing Umidori's opposition.

◇◇◇◇

"Those two are members of the Mud Hat Faction."

A few minutes later, Bullshit-chan was herself again.

Arguably. There were still tear streaks on her cheeks, and her eyes were rather red, but she was focused on the task at hand, no longer concerned about such trifles.

"In this case, Mud Hat is not something they wear on their heads, but the name a person goes by," Bullshit-chan explained, looking at each face in turn. "You've all heard my claims that someone who can't lie is actually an expert fallicider, right?

"Well, if the opposite of a fallicider is a liefluencer, what exactly is their deal?"

"……A liefluencer?" Umidori said, frowning. "That word tells me nothing."

"He's a hypnotist."

"……A what now?"

"A hypnotist, Umidori. A practitioner of hypnosis. A man who can make you sweat even in a cold room, who can knock you right out merely by saying, '*You are feeling very sleepy.*' You know the drill! I'm sure you've seen that ilk on TV before."

Bullshit-chan appeared to be totally serious.

"That is not a power to be underestimated. The ability to manipulate hearts and minds, to bend them to your will—it's actually got quite a bit in common with your candor claymore, Umidori. Actually, the fact that he can control it arguably makes his skill an advanced version of your own."

"......Okay, you've lost me, Bullshit-chan," Nara said, clearly not buying this. "Where's this coming from? It's not like I'm an expert on hypnotists, but aren't they just con artists?"

"No, Nara, they are not. Hypnosis itself is a viable technique with a lengthy history. At the very least, I am personally acquainted with a human who genuinely *can* hypnotize people.

"And that hypnotist calls himself Mud Hat. Naturally, it isn't his real name. Everything about him is a mystery—his name, his age, his origins, and his history. All we know is that he appears to be a tall, gaunt, Japanese man. And that he's a hypnotist specializing in the Belied."

Bullshit-chan paused to exhale.

"Think about it. If a hypnotist can make someone cold think they're hot—and someone wide awake fall asleep—then they can take a Beliar's desire, amplify its strength, and force it to the necessary threshold. Imagine what someone doing that could achieve."

"......F-force it to the threshold?" Umidori gasped, blinking. "Th-that sounds bad! If someone like that really exists, Beliars would be falsifying the world all the time!"

"Exactly, Umidori. That's what's so scary about it. And doing that is well within Mud Hat's capabilities," Bullshit-chan said, scowling. "That man's very voice is *unnatural*. Just listening to him talk puts you at ease, gets you drunk on the sound of it. It's very distinctive. He whispers a few things to you and they all sink deep into your heart—and then the next thing you know, your feelings are infinitely stronger. Apparently. I've never actually been hypnotized by him, so this is all secondhand."

"......Huh. Well, if he can actually do that, he's the ideal partner for any Beliar." Nara nodded. "So what does this Mud Hat want in return? When he hypnotizes a Beliar, do they have to pay him?"

"Quite the opposite, Nara. Mud Hat doesn't care at all about money.

"With a power like his, he can easily make more money than he could possibly use. This man requires only one thing in return—the right to observe a Beliar's actions firsthand."

"......I don't get it," Nara said, tilting her head. "The right to observe? What value could that possibility have?"

"According to him, it's front-row seats to the human spectacle."

"......The human spectacle?"

"'How the Beliars think, what choices they make, and what that leads to. Observing all this is a spellbinding experience, similar to 'the elation you feel at the end of a really great movie.' That was how he once described it to me.

"Basically, Mud Hat hypnotizes the Belied for *fun*. It's his hobby; he goes around helping people falsify the world for shits and giggles, for his own amusement."

"......Falsifying the world for fun? This guy's a public menace," Nara scoffed. "Not that I'm one to talk."

"Mud Hat tends to gather a pack of Beliars—he calls them clients. His hypnosis allows them to strengthen their lies, and Mud Hat gets to spectate on their lives from close at hand. It's arguably a mutually beneficial arrangement.

"And all cards on the table, I used to be part of that group—a member of the Mud Hat Faction. Maybe one or two years ago?"

Bullshit-chan closed her eyes, as if searching her memory.

"Mud Hat showed up out of nowhere. Found me, revealed his nature, explained his faction, and invited me to join them. 'If you're all alone, you could use some friends.'

"I heard him out, and after due consideration...agreed to join them. I survive by killing lies, so his proposal was extremely appealing."

"How so?"

"Simple, Nara. Just hanging around Mud Hat gave me access to a font of information on the Belied. I no longer needed to scramble all over town hoping to stumble across my next meal. If I only care about keeping myself fed, there's no better environment.

"And fortunately, the rest of the Mud Hat Faction accepted me readily. Their core stance was to accept any and all lies. And Mud Hat not only personally recruited me, he was weirdly fond of me."

"Fond of you? Why?"

"'Long since abandoned by your host, yet you've survived a decade through sheer obstinacy.' My very existence amused him. 'I've never seen a lie as stubborn, brazen, or desperate!' 'As wretched as any human!' From the start, he had a lot of glowing praise."

".......Right, okay. So like those Beliars, you were allowed in the faction to entertain Mud Hat," Nara said, nodding to herself. "I get that logic, but I don't understand this outcome. Bullshit-chan, if you were allowed into the faction, then why are you alone again now?"

".......That's even simpler. I betrayed them." Bullshit-chan's voice dropped low, her expression gloomy. "In other words, after voluntarily asking to join their ranks, I split away from them less than a year later, of my own free will.

"Objectively, I imagine my behavior looks nonsensical. But the situation left me with no choice. Before joining them, I had no clue the Mud Hat Faction's Beliars would be so thoroughly dangerous."

"Dangerous...like that bandage lady?" Umidori asked. "Hurt, was it? From what you've said, she must be part of Mud Hat's faction. She did mention that name, and she called you a former comrade."

"Exactly, Umidori. But she's not one of the Beliars—she's a lie.

"Hurt is a core member of the Mud Hat Faction, a threat to society, and one of the most catastrophic lies around. It's not just her—basically all the core members are equally dangerous."

".......A threat to society?"

"Absolutely. They're societal evils," Bullshit-chan declared. "They don't care who gets hurt as long as they get their way. The brakes of their rational minds have long since broken. They don't have a trace of conventional ethics or morals left. Complete outliers.

"Look at how Hurt acted earlier. Kicking in a door by way of hello, cutting people's feet off, doing whatever she felt like. We were very lucky that only I took direct damage—and I do mean *lucky*. Umidori, Nara—both of you could easily have wound up badly injured."

".................!"

Bullshit-chan's dire statement reminded Umidori of just how chilling Hurt's naked hostility had been.

"Or do you wish to lose your feet like this kitty cat has?"

That had been a clear and transparent threat. If Umidori had taken even a second longer to topple over, she might well not *have* feet.

And if she had not *actually* made good on similar threats, merely stating it aloud could not possibly have carried such force.

"Fundamentally speaking, the Belied do not ordinarily have that much influence on society," Bullshit-chan said, shrugging. "Lies like myself are supposed to function as mere communication tools, if extremely effective ones. Manifestations are an unexpected outcome of this system—like a bug. Even if the occasional aberration—a Beliar— appeared, they would normally vanish like bubbles, unable to falsify the world.

"In other words, manifest lies are but a fleeting dream, a temporarily byproduct of human desperation. At least…that was how it was until a decade ago."

"……But Mud Hat's appearance changed all that?" Nara sighed. "A threat that would never have gotten beyond the pupal stage—if you'll excuse the metaphor—can now become butterflies and flap their wings. All thanks to Mud Hat's hypnosis."

"My point exactly, Nara. No matter the outcome of their actions, Mud Hat will simply be amused—he doesn't care about consequences."

"……And you betrayed the faction to try to prevent that fate?"

"……Basically, yes," Bullshit-chan admitted with some hesitation. "After a year with them, I became alarmed by the threat they posed. I concluded that I couldn't let them go unchecked and decided to turn all my former comrades into my mortal enemies."

"……Huh? That's wild," Envy Sakura said, looking baffled.

She'd been sitting next to Nara, staring into the distance, like none of this interested her at all. Only now did the conversation engage her attention.

"Nothing about you makes sense. After all this time, how does something like that motivate a betrayal?" Envy Sakura was frowning, glaring across the table. "Bullshit-chan, was it? I've been listening to you run your mouth off from inside Yoshino all day, so I *do* get the gist of what your deal is. But since when were you the sort of lie who cares about right and wrong?"

"……………"

"All this time, you've never cared about anything but your own survival. You even ate other lies! It makes no sense for you to suddenly get all concerned about societal evils, about anything other than yourself."

With that, she broke off, sneering.

"Or what, have you grown a conscience after all this time? That'd be *rich*."

"......Hmph, don't be absurd, Envy Sakura," Bullshit-chan said, her grin every bit as condescending. "I assure you, I have nothing resembling a conscience whatsoever. I'm Bullshit-chan. I survived a decade out of sheer obstinance. I have no need of anything that doesn't directly fill my stomach."

"......Then you really don't make sense. If all you care about is eating lies, then you'd be infinitely better off staying with the Mud Hat——"

"No, Envy Sakura. It didn't work like that," Bullshit-chan said, shaking her head. "You see, if we let those people have their way, *the human race will go extinct*."

"......Excuse me?"

"I'm not exaggerating in the slightest. The Beliars Mud Hat has amped up are all *that* dangerous. As of now, they're still lying low, but if they really start to flex, human society won't survive it.

"And if humanity goes extinct, I'm in trouble. With no humans to give lies shape, I can't eat them! I'll starve to death!

"That's why I betrayed the faction, Envy Sakura. Not for world peace, but one hundred percent for my own needs. I declared war on my former comrades purely to keep food on my table."

"......Ha, puh-leez," Envy Sakura said. She snorted, disgusted. "You are a creature of pure gluttony, then? Classic. What a filthy way to live. I can see why that Hurt character called you vermin."

"......Fine, say what you will. I am but a filthy lie. That is a fact beyond argument." Bullshit-chan had clearly decided to own it. "I suppose that brings us to the *real* reason I was after Nara's lie.

"As you're all aware, I'm a small fish in a big sea. Going up against the Mud Hat Faction all on my lonesome would get me nowhere fast. To that end, I decided I needed to strengthen myself—by consuming the lies of Beliars not in the faction already and gaining enough power to go up against them. In other words, when I said I was on the brink of death and going for the long shot, I was talking shit.

"And why did I lie about it? Well, if I start by explaining how dangerous the faction members are, I figured Umidori would freak out and refuse to help."

"................."

Umidori flinched and gave Bullshit-chan a deeply indignant look, but the recipient paid this no attention.

"That said, I didn't expect to have the faction on my heels already. I was certain those powerful Beliars wouldn't even notice if a third stringer like me turned traitor—but clearly, there was an exception, and I totally overlooked that fact."

"......Aha. So this lie calling herself Hurt is the exception?" Nara said, getting ahead of her. "She sure did seem to have it in for you personally, Bullshit-chan."

"Right you are, Nara. Hurt has had it in for me since I first joined the Mud Hat Faction. After all, she's a fundeceptionist."

"A...what now?"

"Hurt believes that lies should consider nothing else, merely serve as tools, faithful to the instinct that drives us to be told. From that perspective, a lie like me—one who has abandoned my original purpose and clings to my individuality—is unacceptable."

Bullshit-chan let out a long, weary sigh.

"We may *seem* like living things, but our true nature is no different than the air around us or the motes of dust floating within it. *'What point is there in clinging to that false life?' 'If your host has discarded you, then you should choose to dissipate and be told by some other humans.'* Hurt bent my ear like that a lot.

"She brandishes that as point of pride. And I stand in direct opposition to everything she's proud of. Naturally, she cannot abide me, and clearly, the moment I left Mud Hat's protection, she saw that as her chance to eliminate me for good, even bringing her own Beliar, Hayakawa, along."

"......What the—? Her pride? That's why she's trying you kill you?" Umidori clearly had objections. "She's insane! If she was just out to punish you for betraying them, at least that would make sense! But murdering someone because you don't like their way of life...?"

"Umidori, I appreciate you saying that, but expecting *human* logic from Hurt is barking up the wrong tree," Bullshit-chan said, shaking her off. "Point is, I'm sunk. Hurt's never gonna let me go. She's one hundred percent out to get me and has no other motives, so there's no room to negotiate.

"And she's a core member of the faction. A weak lie like myself can't even begin to fight back. My only option is to resign myself to my fate."

"......?! D-don't be hasty, Bullshit-chan! You can't just...give up!"

"Don't worry, Umidori. Or you, either, Nara. If she can finish me off, she'll be satisfied and should leave town.

"Hurt may seem like she's got a screw loose, but she's one of the less-unhinged faction members. She might rough humans up a bit but would never dream of taking their lives. She's a die-hard lie. Reducing the number of symbionts capable of telling her? It goes against her very policy. That is now how her pride believes a lie should act.

"She may be the physical embodiment of unreasonableness, but on this one point, on her dedication to her own pride, we can trust her. You'll be fine, Umidori. Even if I die, you can simply go back to your old life, just as you always have."

"......! No, I can't! I do not accept this ending at all!"

"I am hardly in favor of it myself. I didn't expect our fallicidal ambitions to be thwarted so soon." Bullshit-chan shifted uneasily. "But what choice do I have? I risked my life on a long shot, misread the odds, and it blew up in my face. I've already failed. All I can do is resign myself......"

But then...

"——That's not true, Bullshit-chan."

"......Hmm?"

"You *do* have a choice. It's far too soon to give up. Perhaps Umidori will let you act all acquiescent and mosey on off to get yourself killed, but I'm not about to stand for it."

Yoshino Nara.

Her face was as expressionless as ever, but her eyes held a powerful light as they locked on Bullshit-chan.

"I think you seriously need to take a step back from this, Bullshit-chan. Things aren't that desperate. Your death is not guaranteed. Your fear of Hurt has simply blinded you to that fact."

"......Huh?!"

"Think about it. If Hurt is actually coming to kill you, then *we* just need to kill her right back."

"......! Wh-what?!" Bullshit-chan yelped.

Nara didn't bat an eye.

"What I said, Bullshit-chan." She nodded. "Same thing I proposed in Umidori's room. We just need to turn that psycho bitch into your next meal. You, me, Umidori, and Envy Sakura—all working together."

◇◇◇◇

......While they were talking in the restaurant...

A woman in a hospital gown with bandages over her eyes was stalking the Isuzunomiya night, with a brown-haired woman in a long skirt following her.

"——Shit! It took too damn long to heal up! Where'd that kitty cat go?!" Hurt snarled. "Human scum! I make a friendly overture, and she dares turn me down?!"

Nara's attack had clearly left her fuming.

"It hasn't been that long! They can't have gotten far! But that's not the problem..."

Her head spun, and she angrily clicked her tongue.

Everyone around them—young and old, male or female—had the exact same face. It was patently absurd, yet it was the truth.

"This has got to be her lie at work. With her fauxroma spread everywhere, my nose isn't helping! Obnoxious as all get out!"

A vein was throbbing on Hurt's forehead.

"This is a declaration of war, yes?! So be it! I was willing to let you join our faction, but not anymore! That tramp and her lie and the kitty cat are all going straight to hell!"

"...........Um, Hurt?"

Just then, the woman walking with her—Hayakawa—piped up.

"...Are you really going to kill Bullshit-chan?"

"......What?" Hurt said, stopping dead in her tracks and swinging her face around to her Beliar.

"I—I mean, Bullshit-chan used to be one of us. E-even if she betrayed Mud Hat...killing her seems a bit much."

"..............."

For a long moment, Hurt just stared at her, speechless. Then...

"You slug! How dare you take issue with my actions!"

"Urk!"

Hurt's fist came down hard on the top of Hayakawa's head. She let out a short groan and crumpled to the ground.

"Fool! Nitwit! Dullard! Shit for brains! You can't ever ever ever ever do the slightest thing unless I say so, yet you have the nerve to voice your opinions now of all times?! Is it your life's purpose to piss me off?!"

"......! S-sorry! I'm sorry!"

Hurt kicked Hayakawa repeatedly while the Beliar was curled up in a heap, squeaking out apologies.

A spectacle so violent it made the crowd stop and stare.

"——What? You got a problem with this?!"

Hurt's roar sent them scattering. Evidently, they'd decided to stay out of this.

"......Hmph, subspecies," Hurt spat out, watching them flee. Then she looked back down and blinked in surprise. "......What's wrong? What are you doing?"

Hayakawa was still curled up on the ground—but for some reason, her hands were inside her clothes.

Like she was trying to keep them safe from Hurt's kicks.

"......Ha! Hayakawa, do your hands mean that much to you?"

"..............."

"That's hilarious. All this time, and you still think you're a surgeon? Ha, not that I care."

As she spoke, Hurt pulled a little device from her pocket and dropped it in front of Hayakawa.

"Just do your part. That's far more productive than speaking out of turn or pointlessly clinging to your profession."

"......! Th-that's......!"

When she saw the device, Hayakawa's face turned pale.

It was a tape recorder, with earphones attached.

"Give it a listen, Hayakawa."

"..............Mm."

Hayakawa nodded, her expression vacant—like a woman possessed. She put the earphones on and pressed the switch on the recorder, playing the tape's contents.

"......Ah, ahhh! Aughhhhhhh!"

And the moment the sounds hit her eardrums, Hayakawa's expression melted.

"Mud Hat...! Mud Hat...!"

"That's more like it, Hayakawa. Let Mud Hat's hypnosis tape heal your wounded heart," Hurt purred, watching the transformation take hold. "If your desire is elevated even briefly, that strengths my own powers. Now I'm more than a match not just for the kitty cat, but for that pink-haired skank, too."

◇◇◇◇

"Where's all this coming from, Nara?" Bullshit-chan asked, stunned. "Do you really think the four of us can turn the tables on Hurt?"

"Clearly, it's the simplest solution," Nara said, meeting her gaze. "If Hurt's that hell-bent on killing you, then we just have to eliminate *her*. That way, you'll be totally safe! Even a child can understand the logic.

"True, Hurt is a powerful lie. I imagine you'd never stand a chance against her on your own. Maybe this resignation idea *would* be your only option. But if Envy Sakura and I help? That evens the playing field. Both sides have a Beliar. With me in your camp, Bullshit-chan, the odds are no longer dismal. We're equally matched—and this is hardly impractical."

"......W-wait, Nara," Bullshit-chan managed, sounding defeated. "Yes, if you helped me, that would certainly be a far less bleak battle than if I went up against her on my own. But we'd still stand little chance of winning.

"That's simply the difference in the strength of your lies. If we only account for the force of the desire, Nara, the two of you are a solid match for Hurt. You may even be stronger than her! But don't forget, they have Mud Hat's hypnosis up their sleeve."

"......Ah-ha. You mean they got a cheat code, while we have to fight fair. And that puts us at a disadvantage."

"The only reason we managed to get away last time is because you caught Hurt by surprise. We won't get that lucky twice. And by this point, Hurt will have made Hayakawa listen to Mud Hat's hypnosis—she'll have a tape recorder with his voice on it or whatever. With that heightening the Beliar's desire, we ain't gonna win, no matter how you slice it."

"——Listen to the cat! This is madness, Yoshino!" Envy Sakura cried, jumping in. "I hate to agree with her, but on this one point, I've gotta stop you! Clashing with that lie just to save *her*? That's far too risky! And...when you think about it, there's nothing in it for us!"

"......Now, now, calm down, Envy Sakura. No need to raise your voice; I can hear you loud and clear," Nara said, shrugging. "I appreciate your concern, but let's skip do or don't and talk about can or can't. I really don't think the situation is anywhere near as dire as Bullshit-chan says."

With that, Nara turned her gaze to the far side of the table.

"I don't know firsthand how powerful Mud Hat's hypnosis is... But *we've* got Tougetsu Umidori."

"......Huh?" Umidori flinched, blinking at her. "Wh-what? What about me?"

"Puh-leeze, Umidori. Try to follow the conversation. Do you even remember why Bullshit-chan came to see you today? She planned to use your candor claymore to murder my desire and weaken my lie. Right?

"We need merely apply that same logic to weaken Hurt. Give your powers a trial run."

Umidori's eyes swam, but Nara caught her gaze and held it.

"If they're boosting themselves with Mud Hat's hypnosis, then we've simply gotta weaken them to the point where we can win, right? And that was Bullshit-chan's plan all along. We're about to embark on an irregular fallicide."

"......Irregular?"

"The target's no longer me, but that brown-haired lady in the dorky skirt."

As she spoke, Nara turned her poker face to the ceiling.

"What was her name...Hayakawa? Basically, if we can get through to her, then we've as good as won. No matter how strong Hurt is, no lie is a threat when cut off from their energy source. At least, that's how you yourself explained it, Bullshit-chan.

"So at the least, if you could share all the intel you got on Hayakawa? Before you go back to wailing about how you're definitely gonna die. You throw in the towel later."

"..............."

For a long moment, Bullshit-chan waffled, her eyes going every which way. But at last, she let out a sigh, like she'd given up.

"Her name's Itami Hayakawa. She's a doctor."

"She is?!"

"Yes, and not just any doctor. She's a brilliant surgeon, skilled enough to have once worked overseas." Bullshit-chan spoke quietly. "Her gift for surgery is practically synonymous with her very existence. She's in her midtwenties, yet surgeons the world over know her name. They say, '*She was born not to save lives, but to operate.*'"

"......Okay?" Nara said, tilting her head. Clearly baffled by that assessment. "I don't really get that, but I'm assuming she pulled off a bunch of difficult operations?"

"No, Nara." Bullshit-chan shook her head. "Not just difficult operations—any and all. Every type of surgery the world had deemed impossible to pull off—Hayakawa made every one of them a success through raw talent alone."

"......Huh? By every, you mean *all* of them?"

"Yes, every last one. There is no operation Hayakawa cannot perform. As a result, the world we live in no longer contains any 'impossible' procedures. Though that premise requires that Hayakawa hold the scalpel, and in any average medical ward, these surgical feats remain entirely out of reach."

"Back up a minute, Bullshit-chan," Umidori said, frowning. "Is this whole gifted surgeon thing even true? From what I saw in my apartment, that lady didn't seem particularly impressive at all."

"Appearances can be deceptive, Umidori. And she's long since retired."

"Retired?"

"Yes, a few years back. Supposedly, she was a bit more outgoing when she was still active. I only met her after she retired and became a Beliar, so my information's secondhand."

"......Can you even become a surgeon at that age?" Umidori asked. "I had the impression it takes a whole lot of time to be considered a proper doctor. If she's still in her midtwenties, she's clearly way too young."

"Well, she would be. She didn't get her license in Japan. She got it *abroad*."

"Th-that wouldn't make a difference...?"

"There are exceptions, Umidori. Her uncanny gift for surgery got her noticed, and they decided they needed her in the field as soon as possible. She was given a medical license in her teens."

"......Uh, huh? What? That sounds like something out of a manga. Do things like that actually happen?!"

"I don't know; don't ask me. No matter how crazy it sounds, it actually happened, so we've gotta accept it as fact. Point is: A few years back, Hayakawa was considered a twentysomething superstar surgeon, and she was flying all over the world to flaunt her skills. Then one day, without any warning—she abruptly retired."

"......Did she?" Umidori said, frowning. "Why did she do that? Did she botch an operation?"

"No, she never once made a single mistake. But she was forced out of the profession *because* she never made a medical error."

"...........??"

"She did not become a doctor to save lives. She became a doctor purely so she could perform operations.

"That's not entirely unusual. She had a gift for surgery, and she tackled her operations like an athlete would a challenging game. Then one day, she realized there was not a single operation that could entertain her—and that broke her heart."

"......Huh?"

"And so, she told a lie. Said she wanted a surgery that would test her mettle, one even she could not be sure she'd execute successfully. That if she could perform an operation like that, she'd be willing to die for it."

Bullshit-chan let out a sigh, slumping over.

"There are total weirdos out there, in the strangest places. Anyway, that's how Hurt came to be. A lie with the power to do nigh fatal—but not quite fatal—damage to any human or living thing.

"For example, it was her ability that sliced off my feet. Anyone who Hurt attacks will be put at death's door, in a condition so critical that even with Hayakawa's skills…she might not be able to save their lives. And then Hayakawa goes and does just that."

"G-good lord! Making problems just to solve them? She's like that yokai, the *kamaitachi*!" Umidori gasped. Then: "But is that really something she needs the power of lies to accomplish? Legality aside, she could just go around hurting people herself, then patching them up."

"No, she couldn't, Umidori. No injury caused by human hands would ever give Hayakawa trouble. And what she needs isn't just any old massive trauma. Not to be gross, but if you brought her a mangled corpse several days after death, even Hayakawa's not able to reverse the irreversible. She very specifically needs wounds that will be fatal, but where she still has a chance of saving them."

"……Okay, I guess I get that. That's a very thin line, and if you want to repeatedly walk it, you might need a lie," Nara said. She'd been listening in silence, but now her tone was more…impressed. "Hurt's a good name. Functionally, she can give anything alive any injury or illness she wants?"

"Yes, it's every bit as brutal as it sounds." Bullshit-chan nodded gravely. "If Hurt was of a mind to do it, she could give every human in this town a critical injury. The only reason she doesn't is because she stops herself—believing she shouldn't reduce the number of humans capable of telling lies. Without that, Umidori, Nara, and me—we'd all be long since dead."

"Bullshit-chan, I hate to keep hammering this point, but is that really actually true?" Umidori said, clearly unconvinced. "I just can't believe that timid-looking lady is capable of anything this cruel. It doesn't feel right."

"……Mm, that is the question." Bullshit-chan frowned, mulling it over. "Honestly, I've never really spoken to Hayakawa one-on-one, so I'm speculating, but I get the impression she'd rather not be a Beliar."

"She wants out?"

"Quite a few Belied get like that. They nurse a desire for ages, only to find out it's not quite what they hoped it would be when it comes true. Yet they can't quit because Mud Hat's hypnosis is artificially sustaining their desire."

"......Well, one look at how they treated each other, and that much is obvious," Envy Sakura said, breaking her silence. "The lie was clearly in charge, completely flipping the power balance. If the Beliar's a wimp, that'll happen. The total opposite of Yoshino and me."

"But if that's true, then we've got a good shot at this, Bullshit-chan," Nara declared, sounding sure of herself. "If Hayakawa would rather not be a Beliar, then all we've got do is give her a push."

"............"

But Bullshit-chan was giving Nara an uncertain look.

"Not so fast, Nara. I don't get it. You got me blabbing everything about Hayakawa, but...why would you even be making this offer?"

"From your point of view, you just met me today, I talk a lot of shit, and I'm not even human. Not only that, but I was trying to kill your precious lie—you should have it in for me! So why...?"

"Hmph, what a ridiculous question, Bullshit-chan." Nara sighed, exasperated. "How we got here is irrelevant. What matters is that, right now, I want to help you. Or what, Bullshit-chan, would you rather I *wasn't* on your side?"

"......N-no, I wouldn't say that."

"And just to be clear, I'm not doing this for *free*."

"Mm?"

"That should be obvious! I'm not *that* nice. I'm taking on the risk of backing you up here, so if I don't get something in return—it ain't worth it."

"......So what? I mean, there's not really anything I can give you, Nara."

"I don't need a *thing*. Just a promise."

"......A promise?"

"Yes. Promise me you'll make it so Tougetsu Umidori can lie."

"............Huh?"

Bullshit-chan's jaw dropped.

Nara just kept talking.

"You said as much to try to get Umidori on board with your fallicidal plans, right? In which case, you'd better be true to your word. If you're gonna get her involved in this mess, then you *have* to make good. Give her the gift of lies if it costs you your life.

"I'll take a verbal contract for now, but I want you to swear a vow, right here. Bullshit-chan, that will be the one and only thing that makes me help you."

"......Wh-what the—?"

The words had come pouring out of Nara's mouth, but Bullshit-chan's head was clearly spinning.

"Umidori? Umidori again? I guess you've been consistent..."

"Well, yeah. I'm on her side," Nara said. She glanced at Umidori. "No matter what happens, no matter who argues otherwise, no matter what *she* says, if the whole world turns topsy-turvy—I fully intend to stay in Umidori's corner. If it'll help her out, I'm willing to do anything I can."

".............."

Hearing this confused Umidori as much as it did Bullshit-chan.

"......I—I don't get it, Nara," she said, her voice a squeak. "Wh-why would you do all that for me? We haven't even spent that much time together. And I didn't let you get that close! Yet here you are..."

"......I imagine you wouldn't understand," Nara said after a long silence. "I mean, you barely even remember that day one year ago."

"......Huh?"

"Everything you did for me in that *okonomiyaki* shop. I owe you a tremendous debt. If you don't remember that happening, I imagine it's quite strange that I'd go this far for you.

"But well, I know why you don't remember it. I mean, you were hardly in your right mind."

"......??"

"But what do you say, Umidori? I've made my stance clear. But whether we actually go out and fight Hurt is *your* decision."

Nara was very clear on this.

"Honestly, your life *will* be in danger. If Bullshit-chan's right, not killing humans is a point of pride for Hurt—but is that a restriction we can really count on? I wouldn't put too much faith in it. When the chips are down, I imagine Hurt wouldn't hesitate to do fatal damage to us, too.

"So I want you think long and hard on it, Umidori. Do *you* want to save Bullshit-chan? Or should we let her go?"

"..............."

For several seconds, Umidori sat in silence.

All her thoughts and emotions were spinning.

"......I—I think——"

7

Showdown in a Children's Park

"Yes, I planned to do just that. Continuing to work here will never allow me to achieve my goals. I had no intention of renewing my contract with you. We are done."

With that declaration, fifteen-year-old Yoshino Nara left the agency president's office.

But just as she stepped outside…

"——Yoshino!"

A woman in a suit called her name.

"……?!" Nara gulped, surprised to see her. "Mom? Why are you…?"

"I-I'm so sorry, Yoshino! I had a critical thing at work, and it took forever. I didn't make it in time."

She was clearly out of breath. Fortysomething, short reddish hair, a petite build. Very even features—and they bore a close resemblance to Yoshino Nara's own.

"S-so? Yoshino, how'd the meeting go? It's over already?"

"……………"

For a long moment, Nara didn't even attempt to answer her mother's question.

No expression on her face, but a searching look in her eyes.

"……Why'd you come, Mom?" she said at last, sounding vexed. "There's no reason for you to be here. This has nothing to do with you. I can settle this myself; don't butt in."

"......! O-oh, listen to you! How can I not be here? You're still a child, and I'm your guardian!"

As she spoke, Nara's mother moved closer to her.

"A-and I heard loud voices from inside... Did he say something awful to you?"

"..............!"

Her mother sounded genuinely concerned, but Nara just looked the other way.

"Nope! Nothing happened that you need to worry about. I just got fired."

"......Huh?"

"Apparently, they can't afford to keep a 'lunatic' around. He called me an insane, stupid psychopath."

"....................!"

Her mother's face twisted in pain.

"......Yoshino!"

And she ran right over to Nara, throwing her arms around her tiny frame.

"——?! Wh-what are you doing, Mom?!"

"I'm so sorry, Yoshino. I should have been there with you through that pain. You may seem mature, but you're still just a fifteen-year-old girl!"

She was whispering in her daughter's ear, clearly meaning every word.

"But know this, Yoshino. No matter what anyone else says or thinks, your mom and dad will always be on your side, through thick and thin."

".........Huh?"

"It doesn't matter to us what thoughts drive you. That's irrelevant! We both know for a fact that you're a really good girl."

".............."

But in response to her mother's kindness...

"......What the hell?"

"......Hmm?"

"You're on my side? Don't lie to me!"

Bam!

She shoved her mother away with all her might.

"Eek?! Wh-what was that for, Yoshino?!"

"......If you and Dad are *really* on my side," Nara said, dusting herself off, "then why is it you *still* haven't had plastic surgery?"

"......Huh?"

"How many times do I have to say it? You should both have the same face I do! That's the mission God gave me! Yet neither one of you ever listen to a word I say! You don't even try to understand!"

"..............."

Nara's fury left her mother momentarily speechless.

"......L-like I've said before, surgery to have my daughter's face? That doesn't even make sense."

She sounded totally calm, like she was just stating the obvious.

"Huh?! How does it not make sense?! I've explained how it's good for you a thousand times!"

"A-and what doesn't make sense doesn't make sense. I—I am sorry, Yoshino. I just can't wrap my head around anything you say."

"..............!"

"S-still, I mean it, Yoshino. You may have your eccentricities, but we both love you more than anyone else! That one thing is absolutely true!"

"——Enough, Mom! You're so dumb!"

Like a sulky child, Nara cut her off.

"You and Dad are too normal to understand my pain! I won't be home for dinner!"

With that, she fled off down the agency fire escape.

"Ah! Yoshino, come back here!"

"Wahh... *Sniff, sniff!*"

——Leaving a trail of teardrops in her wake.

That same evening...

Yoshino Nara was sniveling on a bench by the station.

"——So dumb! Dumb, stupid, brain-dead!"

Paying no attention to the crowds moving past her, her eyes on empty air, she continued to vent.

"They're all idiots!"

But no matter how she gnashed and moaned, the muscles in her face never once moved.

"......I'm hungry," she whispered after a good long cry. It was getting pretty late. But after what she'd said before she ran off, she couldn't exactly go home. She felt like getting something nice and filling. Like her favorite food, *okonomiyaki*.

"——Uh, hey, Nara? You okay?"

But then, a girl's voice sliced across the void of Nara's mind. A girl she didn't recognize.

Surprised, Nara looked up, examining the speaker.

"..............Who are you again?"

Those words spilled out on pure reflex. Looking closer, she did have an inkling that she'd seen this girl somewhere before. The girl *was* wearing the same uniform as Nara—so did that mean she was a classmate of hers at Isuzunomiya High, her brand-new school?

The girl was tall, and her face was not that bad. Naturally, it was no match for Nara's, but by the general standards of this world, she would likely qualify as pretty cute. Long, glossy black hair down to her waist. But her most impressive feature was the sheer size of her boobs.

"............."

For a moment, Nara found herself unable to tear her eyes away from them.

Was she padding her bra? That rack was obviously larger than average, so she genuinely had to wonder. But they seemed weighty—like they were about to tear through the girl's blazer. At the agency she'd recently belonged to, even their pin-up models didn't have chests this ginormous.

Despite herself, Nara looked down at her own chest. A gentle slope, one that posed no obstacle to the view of her feet. This alone made it hard to believe the two girls were wearing the same uniform.

——At this point, her train of thought dragged up the memory. The class had all done introductions right after the opening ceremony, and there'd been one girl with a weird name—and breasts out to here.

"Oh, right, I've seen you somewhere... Class? Uh... You had an unusual name?"

◇◇◇◇

"I finally found you, kitty cat."

Hurt's cold voice echoed through the spring night.

In a few hours, the date would change. This was a children's park, a decent distance from any station—populated only by a handful of girls.

Hurt, Itami Hayakawa, Bullshit-chan, Yoshino Nara—and Envy Sakura.

"That redhead Beliar certainly made you hard to find, but judging by the defiance in your eyes, you haven't come to surrender yourself."

"................."

Bullshit-chan had her cat-ear hoodie pulled low over her face and was silently glowering at Hurt from within.

"Hmph, a charmless beast. Didn't you have another human with you before? Where'd she go? I don't see her anywhere in the park."

"Umidori's taken refuge elsewhere," Nara said, flatly answering the question. "She's a regular human, not a Beliar—we can't exactly let her face a dangerous lie like you."

"——Ha! Please. You think *I* would stoop to harming a defenseless human?" Hurt scoffed. "Didn't the kitty cat explain anything? I've never once killed a human. Though I've inflicted my share of pain upon them. That is the nature of my power. Many humans I've encountered may still be confined to bed, but none of them have *died*. That is my pride as a lie—I would never kill someone capable of telling us."

As Hurt spoke, Itami Hayakawa stood in silence, and Hurt pulled her into an embrace.

"And no matter how dangerous a situation I'm walking into, I would never let Hayakawa leave my side. We're together twenty-four seven, three hundred and sixty-five days a year—even in the bath! For the simple reason that I do not trust this woman farther than I can throw her. That's why she's with me now. The best way to keep her out of harm's way is to leave her at my side."

"..............."

In Hurt's arms, Itami Hayakawa's eyes were hollow. She said not a word.

"Whatever—the time for idle prattle is done. Human, you may be a powerful Beliar, but if you choose not to ally yourself with us, then I need merely eliminate our enemy. Send your lie and that kitty cat to the great beyond. Say your prayers!"

"You're the one praying, Bandage Bitch!" Envy Sakura growled, striking first.

With that howl, she generated blades before her, just like last time. They all shot toward Hurt.

A surprise attack, too fast for the eye to follow. Hurt didn't try to dodge, just soaked them all, one after the other slicing into her flesh. But...

"Don't imagine this'll go the same way," she said.

Those blades had cut her all up and down—yet she was *unharmed*.

"While you were sulking about, I had plenty of time to deploy Mud Hat's hypnosis. And you're about to find out just how powerful a boost that is."

As she spoke, she thrust both arms toward Envy Sakura—and several giant bandages appeared in front of her.

"You're no match for me, Pink Hair!"

At her cry, the bandages shot toward Envy Sakura.

"Eek?!"

In mere moments, they'd wrapped themselves around all her long limbs, tying her up.

"......〰〰!!"

Tightly bound, she could no longer move at all.

"——Whew, and the kitty cat never posed a threat. I'll start with you, Pink Hair. I've gained a huge advantage, but you're still trouble with a capital T."

"——! Ahhhhhh......!" Envy Sakura shrieked, the bandages squeezing her hard.

"——Envy Sakura!" Nara came running in, and her lie grimaced, forcing a smile.

"......! I'm fine, Yoshino......! I can handle this!" she insisted. "Honestly, I have no clue why I've got to do all this for that cat, Yoshino, but if you give the word, I'll do everything I can."

She was generating more blades in the air and sending them Hurt's way. But no matter how many blades pierced her flesh, Hurt's smile never wavered—like she was taking zero damage at all.

"Ha-ha-ha! Your host made a stupid decision. If you come to Mud Hat's side, you can be as strong as I am—perhaps even far stronger!"

"............"

But as Hurt cackled, someone was sneaking up behind her.

The ears of her hoodie wobble as she tiptoed to Hurt's side—where Itami Hayakawa stood.

Then—

"Hmph, clever."

"Gah!"

Bullshit-chan's attempted sneak attack came out of nowhere; Hurt's bandages lashed out unexpectedly, sending her flying.

"Did you think you could make a move while I was busy with Pink Hair, kitty cat?"

"..............!"

"Tough luck. Your plan was all too obvious."

Bullshit-chan was writhing on the ground, and Hurt didn't even turn to look, just heaping scorn on her over her shoulder.

"You were after Hayakawa from the start. That is the sole means you have of overcoming the difference in our combat skills. If you can take her hostage, I would be helpless—and so the two of you worked together to slip past me."

Hurt's lips twisted in a sneer.

"But a plan that feeble would never work on me. Do you have any idea how many problems this dead weight has caused for me? Even with the redhead's fauxroma blanketing the town and blinding my nose, I know your scent, kitty cat. All too well. I can sniff you out anywhere, anytime!"

"——!! ∧∧∧ ?!" Flat on the ground, face twisted in pain, Bullshit-chan glared up at her. "......Hayakawa, are you fine with this?!"

"......Huh?"

Itami Hayakawa had been staring vacantly at empty space, but she jumped at the sound of her name, turning to look at Bullshit-chan.

"At the beck and call of your own lie, forced to stay a Beliar via Mud Hat's hypnosis! Is that what you really want?"

"............"

"You'd rather quit this whole Beliar thing! Go back to being a normal human! But if you don't turn on Hurt, that'll never be anything more than a vain hope! You'll be stuck like this the rest of your life!"

"..............I don't care."

"Huh?"

"Nothing matters anymore. Whether I'm a Beliar or not...it won't make a difference," Hayakawa said, shaking her head. "I've already gone too far. The moment I started hurting people, I gave up my right to be a doctor. I have no choice—I'll be a Beliar as long as I live.

"When I was a surgeon, the people around me swore I wasn't a doctor, just a woman who loves doing operations. I always insisted I really was a doctor—but I was just fooling myself. They were right all along. To get what I want, I think nothing of hurting people. I have no right to practice medicine."

She sounded thoroughly anguished.

"The moment I became aware of this, everything else stopped mattering. I'm sorry, Bullshit-chan. I can't stop being a Beliar. And I can't save you all from Hurt."

".........! Hayakawa! You don't——!"

"——Bwah-ha-ha-ha-ha! Your plan has failed, kitty cat!"

Bullshit-chan looked utterly defeated, and Hurt's smile could not have been broader.

"Trying to persuade this woman is utterly futile! She's long past the point of listening to anyone! What now, kitty cat? Don't tell me you're out of ideas already?"

"............∧∧∧!!"

"Ha-ha, really? That was far too easy. I thought you'd at least make it fun, but this is just sad. I can't believe you wimps dared take a run at me," Hurt crowed. She cracked her neck. "Well, I need merely finish you off. Should I go back to my original plan and kill the kitty cat first? Or should I take out Pink Hair before her, prove she has no chance of surviving this, and savor her desperation? Oh, what a difficult decision."

Half her face might have been hidden by bandages, but they did nothing to hide her shit-eating grin. Nothing gave her greater pleasure than holding Bullshit-chan's life in the palm of her hand, imagining the best way to murder her.

——But.

"No, you haven't won yet, Hurt," Nara asserted quietly. She'd been watching the lies face off this whole time. "I know you're having fun bullying Bullshit-chan, but before you proceed, perhaps you should look around."

"......What?" At last, Hurt turned her head. "......Huh?"

Her smile froze.

"H-Hurt!" Itami Hayakawa wailed, clearly terrified. The tip of a four-inch-long kitchen knife was aimed directly at her throat.

"——D-don't move, Hurt!" yelled the black-haired high school girl holding the knife. "I-if you move a muscle, there's no telling what I'll do to this lady! I-I'm not lying!"

"......What's going on? How are you here? How did you get that close to her without me noticing?"

"Did those bandages on your eyes blind you?" Tougetsu Umidori said, clearly rather worked up. "Y-you oughtta be more careful. You seem very confident in your sense of smell, but not everyone out there has a fauxroma. There are humans like me who cannot tell a lie."

"......Huh?" Hurt just gaped at her. "You *can't* lie? That's ridiculous! All humans are liars!"

"L-listen to me! A-as you can see, your host's life is in my hands......!"

Umidori's face was no longer the same as Yoshino Nara's. It had reverted back to her original features. All that pain inflected upon Envy Sakura had made it difficult for her to sustain the falsification.

"If you try to attack me, I'll do it! I don't know how nasty your infliction powers are but look where we stand! You can't get me before my knife reaches Hayakawa's neck!"

".............."

Hurt did not respond to her words at all. For a long beat, she just stood there.

At last, her lips parted.

"Hmph, curious. You really don't smell. That makes no sense at all, but you did get the drop on me, so I have to accept it.

"And? Now that you've got Hayakawa hostage, what do you want from me?"

"......Huh?"

"If you want to get rid of me, then you need merely stick that knife in Hayakawa's throat. The fact that you haven't means you want to negotiate—with her life as collateral."

Hurt rolled her eyes, exasperated.

"Let me guess. Spare the kitty cat, let her go? Lord…you and Red Hair. Why do you even care? I've no idea what's between you, nor do I care, but you're total strangers! Did she share her sob story and get her hooks in you?"

"……! Wh-why are you so confident? Your life is in my—"

"Oh, I appreciate that fact. Hayakawa is my lifeline, and the fool is in enemy hands. You've got a knife to her throat. I am in mortal peril."

Hurt's lips twisted in a smile.

"But what of it? Do you really think you can actually slit her throat?"

"——Huh?"

Hurt clearly didn't think she could, and that made Umidori frown.

"——?!"

And a moment later, that frown gave way to surprise.

Thick fluids started oozing from Hayakawa's throat, spreading out over Umidori's knife.

"Wh-what the……?!"

"You humans are so unsalvageably stupid. Lies do not naturally *have* flesh—I'm sure the kitty cat told you that much. Yet you're still bamboozled by what your eyes tell you. I never once claimed *this* was my main body or the whole of me.

"I don't trust my host one iota, and I would never leave her side for even a second! I keep a portion of myself inside her at all times. And if anyone tries to threaten her, I can instantly spring to her defense—like so."

Hurt snapped her fingers.

A number of tentacles shot out of Hayakawa's body, running through Umidori at prodigious speeds.

"——Umidori?!" Nara shrieked, horrified.

"…………Gah!"

Umidori crumpled to the ground, coughing up blood. She didn't mean to let go of the knife, but it slipped from her fingers.

"Too bad, human. You caught me off guard for an instant, and I admire that—but I was one step ahead."

As she spoke, Hurt was advancing toward her, heels clicking.

"Even if you hadn't tried to negotiate but had merely gone directly for the kill—or attacked Hayakawa in your room while I was down—the outcome would have been the same. I am never not keeping an eye on Hayakawa's safety. You underestimated just how little I trust her. And therein lies your defeat."

"..................!"

"——Now then, with that crisis averted, what am I to do with you?"

Hurt stopped and loomed over Umidori, twisting her lips in a sadistic smirk.

"You may not have succeeded in doing any harm to me, but you did turn your blade on my host. For that, you must be punished."

She stomped on Umidori as hard as she could.

"......! Aughhhhhhhhh?!"

"Heh-heh, I've never been so ashamed in all my life. For a human to get the best of me, if only for an instant? I'm a firm believer in not killing humans, but you've convinced me I should bend that rule this time......!

"Critically, you appear to be unable to tell a lie. That should not be possible, but given the utter lack of fauxroma from you, I have to assume it's true. Heh-heh-heh, what a mess. I don't believe in taking the life of any symbionts capable of telling us, but that rule doesn't apply to a human who *can't*."

"....................!"

"In other words, I don't have a single reason *not* to kill you. Still, that doesn't mean I *have* to. I'm only really after that kitty cat; and I do hear slaughtering living humans can lead to lots of paperwork.

"......So let's do this. Listen, human—swear right here and now that you're *abandoning* the kitty cat. Apologize from the bottom of your heart for going up against me."

"......Swear? Apologize?"

"If you cannot lie, that means your words will be true. You will have genuinely cut the kitty cat loose, and your remorse will be sincere. If you are willing to stoop to both—well, I'm no devil. I wouldn't mind sparing your life."

"..........."

"So what'll it be? Not that I imagine it bears much thought."

Hurt seemed convinced she'd already won, and Umidori listened to her speech with a mind half blurred. Her entire body hurt, and that was only getting worse as time went on. It was a wonder she hadn't passed out yet. Normal high school girls almost never encountered pain of this magnitude unless they, say, got hit by a truck.

Agony, fear, desperation—that would have broken any normal mind, made her submit to any request. If she had, no one would have blamed her for it. Tougetsu Umidori was just sixteen, and she was putting her life on the line for a girl she barely knew.

"............."

And yet, Umidori...

"......N-no way." Face twisted in pain, sweat running down her brow, but a fire burning in those eyes. "I'd rather die than say any of that!"

"......What?"

"I mean, I came here knowing all this! I'm not about to take this deal *now*! Are you a complete idiot?!"

She was shouting, as if her pain didn't matter.

"......Huh? You call *me* an idiot? You dare treat *me* like a fool?"

"Y-yeah, you're the dumbest dumbo in dumbo town! Do I have to say it again? I b-bet throwing your power around and tormenting the weak must feel real good, but Bullshit-chan knows how weak she is, and she still tried to tackle stronger foes—and that's just badass! At the very least, I'd never dream of calling her way of life wretched!"

".............You take that back, human!"

The smile had vanished from Hurt's lips.

"You make it sound like I'm inferior to this kitty cat. Rephrase that at once! Or else—"

"......! No. Come on, you're clearly inferior," Umidori said, smiling desperately, looking up at Hurt. "I mean, think about it. Your lie is just *sad*."

"......Huh?" Hurt's cheeks quivered. "What did you say?"

"L-lies only exist to effect a change upon the world, right? By that standard, Nara's is pretty amazing. She wants to make everyone on earth look the same! Her lie changes the very nature of the world! P-put aside whether that's a *good* idea—you gotta admit it's got scale.

"But what about you, Hurt? You just take people who aren't actually sick, make them sick, and then fix them? You might as well not exist at all! That's just sad. A totally vapid lie. A whole lot of effort for nothing at all."

"..............H-how dare you!" Hurt hissed, veins about to pop. "You have no right! The nerve! The audacity! You call my lie sad? Vapid? Fuck you! Take that back this instant! Say you're sorry!"

"I'm not taking anything back! Nor will I be saying sorry."

Hurt was clearly beside herself, but Umidori just kept winding her up.

"You know it's true. I can't lie. I can't say anything I don't actually think. From the bottom of my heart, I think you suck. And I literally can't say anything else."

"..............!〰〰〰!"

"B-but look how rattled you are. Did I hit the nail on the head? Have you been nursing a sore spot about your own lie? In that case, wow, that must be the pits. And you know if I can say *that*, I actually mean it."

She just kept fanning those flames. And for a long moment, Hurt smoldered in silence—but then her brow furrowed.

"......F-fine! Have it your way! Prepare to die, human!"

She gave a screech so shrill it hurt the ears, and there came a squelching sound from Umidori's stomach.

"——Hrk!"

"I've just crushed several organs. The damage is fatal. There's no saving you now... But I won't be delivering a final blow just yet. First, I'm going to take my time, torment you, make you regret mocking me......!"

Blood spilled from Umidori's lips, and Hurt cackled in pleasure. "Heh-heh-heh... You know, now that I think about it, maybe it's *good* I met a human like you. For a long time now, I've been longing to kill one of you."

"...........Ah, ah...," Umidori gasped, gazing at the blood spilling out of her mouth. "I... I'm really gonna die?"

"Yes, you will. A richly deserved death."

"...........N-no, I don't wanna die!" Umidori whispered, eyes hollow. "I-it hurts so much... I can't breathe... I'm scared... I don't wanna die! Help! Somebody, help me...!"

"——Ha! A bit late for *that*. Begging for your life *now*? That ship has sailed!

"Nobody can save you! Not you, not the kitty cat, not Pink Hair—and fuck it, I'm gonna kill Pink Hair's host while I'm at it! You brought this on yourselves; you made me feel like this, so for once, I'm gonna cast aside my pride and kill all the humans I want! Ha-ha! Ha-ha-ha! Ha-ha-ha-ha-ha-ha-ha!"

. . . .

"......Mm?"

But Hurt's maniacal laugh did not last long.

"......Wh-what the...?" She gasped, gazing at the blood gushing out of her own mouth.

She crumpled to the ground, like the strength had drained from her.

"Wh-what's going on? I can't even stand...? Why...?"

"——Whew, you fell for it, Hurt."

Tougetsu Umidori got to her feet and looked down at her.

She was completely uninjured. As if her wounds had been a *lie*.

"Our plan worked—we win."

◇◇◇◇

"I... I'm really gonna die?" Umidori's voice.

Hurt's attack had left her life a candle in the wind.

"Yes, you will. A richly deserved death."

She gazed down at Umidori and her ruptured organs, a sadistic smile on her lips.

"............N-no, I don't wanna die!" Umidori whispered, eyes hollow. "I-it hurts so much... I can't breathe... I'm scared... I don't wanna die! Help! Somebody, help me...!"

"——Ha! A bit late for *that*. Begging for your life *now*? That ship has sailed!"

Hurt's voice was upbeat, merry. Delighted to hear Umidori plead with her—but Umidori was never looking at Hurt.

She *was* begging for help—but not from *Hurt*.

". . . . ."

At first, Itami Hayakawa had been gazing at Umidori, her expression devoid of life. As if Umidori's desperate pleas were none of her business.

——But that wasn't a problem. Even if she wasn't listening, even if Umidori's voice failed to reach her, she need only *see* her lips move. That got the message across.

Perhaps the other words were lost, but Itami Hayakawa had seen people mouth *help* more than any other word—and she could read those lips.

"…………Ah!"

The significance dawned on her.

She *knew*… And a change swept over her. That hollow look became replaced with a spark.

"Oh, oh, oh…!"

And that alone told Umidori that their plan had *worked*.

——Not long after, all Umidori's pain was gone.

"……Phew." She sighed and stood up.

With a thunder of footsteps, another girl ran over and threw her arms around her.

"Umidori!"

It was Yoshino Nara.

"Whoa… H-hey, Nara, what's up?"

"……That was so hard to watch, Umidori…!"

Nara had her face buried in Umidori's chest, clearly still beside herself.

"I—I knew this was the plan all along, but when Hurt ripped you up and stomped on you, it was all I could do not to throw myself at her…!"

"……Nara," Umidori said, gently rubbing her head.

She'd been all alone, stifling her panic, watching things play out.

Then Umidori's eyes narrowed, and she looked down at Hurt.

"You fell for it, Hurt. Our plan worked—we win."

"——Wh-what?" Hurt gasped, scrabbling in the dirt. "Hayakawa…! Wh-why'd you cut off your desire? Wh-what's going on?"

"……I'm sorry, Hurt," Hayakawa said, standing back, eyes downcast. "It's just, this girl asked for *help*."

"......Huh?!"

"A girl who can't lie, in agony, begging for help because she doesn't want to die? I'm a doctor; I can't let that pass."

"Th-that's the stupidest thing I've ever heard!"

Hurt's voice rose into a shout, clearly comprehending nothing.

"Y-you aren't a doctor! Did you forget how much pain I've caused?! You yourself said you no longer had a right to practice medicine!"

"......Oh, I know all that. But even if I don't have the *right*, that doesn't mean I can just *let* a girl die right in front of me."

Her words were faltering, insecure—yet there was an obstinance lying underneath them.

"A-at the very least, this time, that was the only option. If we'd called an ambulance, she'd have died before it got here. And if I tried to operate myself—well, this isn't exactly an operating room. The only way I had of saving her was to steal your power, Hurt."

"..............!〜〜〜〜〜〜〜!" Hurt bit her lip, then roared, "This was your plan all along?!"

"Totally." Umidori nodded. "Thank you so much, Hurt. I'm so glad you tried to kill me."

"......Th-that doesn't even make sense! This was your *plan*?! How much of it?! Were you just pretending I had you cornered?!"

"None of that was pretend. I can't lie! I couldn't ever deceive anyone that way. I was legitimately at my wit's end.

"We decided ahead of time that since I don't reek of lies, I could sneak up on Hayakawa, put a knife to her throat, take her hostage—then intentionally blow it, setting you up to try to kill me."

"......You *wanted* me to kill you?!"

"Basically, murder was the one line Itami Hayakawa couldn't cross. No matter how much you've got her beaten down, no matter how powerful Mud Hat's hypnosis is, if you cross that line, it all comes tumbling down. You really stepped in it!

"You said you've never once taken a life—and you seemed convinced that was a point of pride. But in fact, you simply unconsciously understood that breaking that rule would lead to your own destruction."

"..................!"

"All we had to do was get you to cross that line. I'm an exception to the wording of your 'pride,' so it wasn't too hard to convince you to kill me. Of course, if I rolled up and said, '*Go on, murder away!*' you'd get suspicious. That would be an obvious trap. So we had to manufacture a situation where killing me would feel like a natural choice.

"In that sense, Nara, Bullshit-chan, and Envy Sakura all played their part. They made it so you just assumed I was taking Hayakawa hostage while they had you occupied—you assumed that was our plan.

"The really hard part was sealing the deal. Like you yourself said, just because you *could* kill me didn't mean you *had* to. That's why I wound you up. The more things I said to piss you off, the more I fanned those flames, the more likely you'd *want* me dead."

"......So you manipulated me into it? With mere words?!"

"Words alone were more than enough. I mean—I can't lie. When I hurl insults, you know I mean every single thing, from the bottom of my heart. You're a proud lie and think you're better than everyone else—so you'd hardly stand for that."

Umidori paused to smile.

"That's the candor claymore. That's what Bullshit-chan calls it—the girl you hate so much."

◇◇◇◇

"That was so reckless, Umidori!" Bullshit-chan said once she'd recovered enough to stand. "Honestly, when you proposed this plan in the restaurant, I thought it was nuts. Way beyond a tightrope act! More like you planned to fall off the tightrope! Can't believe you thought it up."

"......Is that a compliment, or are you talking shit?"

"Pure praise! Your plan is what led us to victory. But I also have regrets."

"Oh?"

"I really should never have agreed to a plan this foolhardy."

Bullshit-chan shook her head.

"In an act of fallicide, my role is to shield you from physical harm, Umidori. After all, you're only human. When you proposed the plan, the sheer audacity of it got me, and I went along with it—but in hindsight, I really shouldn't have. I fully intend to ensure there isn't a next time."

She sounded like she was making a promise to herself. Then she turned to Hurt.

"That said, time we drop the curtains on this fallicide."

".......! W-wait!" Hurt wailed, scrabbling on the ground. "Y-you win! You've got this one! I swear you'll never see me again! Just d-don't..."

".......Don't what?" Bullshit-chan asked, her face a blank slate. "You think I'm gonna let you go? After all this, Hurt? Hayakawa's already cut you loose. Even if I *did* let you go, you wouldn't last long."

She knelt down next to Hurt, peeling the bandages off her eyes.

"Urgh...," she groaned—and her full face was revealed.

——A young woman, midtwenties, still with rather a baby face.

"Y-you have no right! You're not worthy!"

"Er, um...Bullshit-chan, are you really going to eat her?" Umidori said, eyes on Hurt's face, clearly uncomfortable. "Eating...means she'll die, right?"

"Yes, but I think there's a misunderstanding here, Umidori," Bullshit-chan said, turning to face her. "I've certainly said *murder* rather a lot, but *eating* a lie doesn't mean the lie itself actually dies."

"Oh?"

"It simply means that Hurt will become part of *my* body. She'll be entirely under my control—but her mind will remain her own. It's less *eat* than *absorb*, I guess?"

"——Y-you nitwit! That's the *problem*!" Hurt screamed, interrupting her. "Abandoned by my host, losing my flesh—so be it! I need merely find another human to tell me! But if I'm part of you?! Then nobody will be able to tell me again! That's means a lie is as good as dead!"

Even as she spoke, her eyes turned to Itami Hayakawa, a pleading look.

"H-Hayakawa! Please, help me! I've got no one else to turn to!"

"I'm sorry, Hurt," Hayakawa said, shaking her head. "I've made up my mind. I want to be a doctor again. I want to save people. I want to stop being a Beliar—and so I can't choose to help you."

"——! H-Hayakawa! You ungrateful bitch! Do you even understand how hard I've worked for you?! Gah!"

As Hurt began to hurl invectives, Bullshit-chan pinned down her throat, silencing her.

"Give it up, Hurt. You're done."

"......! F-fuck! Shit! God dammit!"

"But don't worry. Your friends will be joining you soon. Inside my stomach!" Bullshit-chan purred, right in Hurt's ear. "You know perfectly well I'm a pseudo-human, not fit to call myself a lie. I'm scared to die—and for that one sad reason, I've spent a decade consuming other lies. True scum. I choose this way of life, and I'll accept any insult hurled at me on account of it without a word.

"But at the same time, I'll do *anything* for my next meal. The Mud Hat Faction is a threat to human society—so I will annihilate you, even if it costs me my life. I'm just that much of a glutton. I will not let you have the humans."

"......! Y-you really think you can win......?!"

Hurt glared back at Bullshit-chan, their noses almost touching.

"A runt like you? Against every member of the faction? You think you can survive that?"

"......Hmph, a stupid question, Hurt." Bullshit-chan snorted. "The die is cast. Win or lose, live or die—the time for those considerations is long since past. Now I need merely scramble. Make the best of things. Go with the flow. Struggle——

"—and fling some bullshit around."

"................!"

"That's all there is to say. You're lunch, Hurt."

And with that—

—their first fallicide concluded.

8

Tougetsu Umidori and Yoshino Nara

"Thank you for joining me today, Umidori," Nara said.

She was using a metal spatula to split up the *modanyaki* (*okonomi-yaki* with noodles in it) on the grill in front of them.

"I come here with my family sometimes, but it's not exactly the type of place for a teenager on their own. If you hadn't come with, there'd have been no *modanyaki* for me tonight."

Like she said, this shop's vibe was less *restaurant* than *bar*. Most seats were filled with grown-ups in suits, fresh from work. Nara and Umidori were at the counter, but they were the only uniformed high school girls here. Meanwhile, Umidori—

"……Wh-what do I do, what do I do, what do I do? I'm eating eating eating out with a girl from class…!"

——was muttering to herself frantically, looping a lot, just quietly enough that Nara couldn't quite make it out. There was *modanyaki* in front of her, but she didn't even reach for the spatula and seemed unlikely to eat a bite.

"……Yo, Umidori, you okay?"

Umidori's condition was genuinely worrying, and Nara didn't let it pass.

"If you're really feeling sick, I guess you could leave now…"

"……! N-no, I'm fine, Nara!"

Umidori shook her head emphatically.

"You were nice enough to invite me—I've come this far; I'm in for the whole shebang!"

She snatched up the cup on the counter and downed the entire contents, as if that would help her get it together.

"——Bwah! O-okay, let's dig in!"

With that, she finally grabbed a spatula and faced her meal. She cut up the *modanyaki*—with far less practiced ease than Nara had demonstrated. Then she scooped a piece up with the spatula and attempted to deliver it straight to her mouth.

"Mm-hmm! That's good, Nara! Scrumptious!"

"……Y-yeah? Glad to hear it."

Nara's face didn't move, but her eyes looked rather startled.

"……Not gonna touch that one. Umidori, there's something I'd like to run by you."

"Oh?" Surprised by that lead-in, Umidori head swiveled her head ninety degrees to face her. "You do?"

"Yeah. You can eat while we talk, but lend me your ears."

With that, Nara launched into a speech.

………………

"——and after fleeing the agency, I found myself on that station bench."

A few minutes later…

Nara had told her *everything*.

The real reason she'd become a model, the problem she'd caused, and why she'd been fired. Full confession, nothing held back.

"So I'm sorry, Umidori. When I said I was too hot to land gigs, that… well, that was true, but it wasn't why I got let go. The reason they fired me was entirely because of this ideal I cling to.

"As to why I lied about it… Honestly, I thought if I told you everything, it would creep you out, and you wouldn't come out to eat with me."

The whole time she spoke, Nara never once looked at Umidori.

She kept her eyes facing forward, never checking her listener's response, not even waiting for a grunt of acknowledgment, just letting the words pour out of her.

"……I just really wanted to eat *with* someone today," she said forlornly. "For this brief moment, I didn't want to be alone. That's why I half dragged you in here when you spoke to me at the station."

Nara herself couldn't fully explain this feeling.

She wondered what was she hoping to gain by sharing all this.

She barely knew this girl. Telling her all this would just alarm her.

She'd get called crazy again.

"Bad luck for you, Umidori. Getting your ear bent like this by a near-total stranger... Admit it: You think I've got a screw loose."

At long last, Nara looked at Umidori again.

Assuming she'd find a look of horror. Half convinced she'd ruined everything.

But instead...

"......Huh?"

...Nara didn't actually get to see the look on Umidori's face.

——Before her eyes could fall on it, Umidori's palm flew in, slapping Nara across the cheek.

"............Huh?"

Stunned, her cheek throbbing, Nara looked again.

"I've heard your story, Nara!" Tougetsu Umidori said.

Her face was bright red. With sheer, unbridled fury.

Her eyes turned all the way up, narrowed like daggers, piercing Nara.

"All I can say is this—call your mom right now and say you're sorry!"

"......Huh? D-did you just...hit me?!"

The realization finally sank in.

"——∧∧∧∧! I—I can't believe it! How could you, Umidori?" Even now, Nara's face remained perfectly still, but her voice was pure fury. "Y-you? Hit me? If you left a single blemish on my face, how would you ever make up for it?!"

"No idea! Doesn't matter!" Umidori wasn't backing down. "I don't give a damn about your face! You have to call your mom right now! Listen to me—you *have* to apologize!"

"......H-huh?"

The sheer ferocity of this took the wind out of Nara's sails.

Umidori's voice wasn't raised or anything—nobody in the shop had even noticed their argument. But she was *intense* in a way that brooked no argument.

"......Er, um. Umidori, you're acting sort of strange?"

This was an outright transformation, and it got Nara wondering.

Umidori had turned bright red, and the ferocious gleam in her eyes seemed totally out of place on the timid, nervous girl she'd come in with. What exactly had come over Umidori while Nara was monologuing about her life?

The woman sitting next to them called out, "Yo, waiter, I ordered *shochu*? This is water!" but Nara was too focused on Umidori to notice.

"Nara, I am fit to be tied!" Umidori said, shoulders actually shaking. "You're the hottest girl alive? You want to unite all humanity behind your face? That's why you joined the modeling agency and why you got fired? I don't give a damn! My problem is entirely the last part of your story!

"Your mother was so worried about you she took time out of work to be there for you, and you pushed her away? That's awful! The worst thing you could do! You've got to pick up your phone and make things up with her right away, Nara!"

".....Um."

Nara just did not get where this was coming from.

"Wh-what are you talking about, Umidori? I pushed my mom? I'm in the wrong?

".....D-did you even hear what I said? That's the *normal* part! I convinced sixteen people to get plastic surgery so they'd look like me? That's totally deranged, but I thought nothing of it! I'm screwed up in the head! Anyone else alive would have had *some* reaction to that... But you've got nothing? You don't give a shit?"

"Yeah, none of that matters. I really just don't care."

Umidori was quite firm on that point.

"——Or I suppose I should say: I can wrap my head around it? I just don't really think what you've done is all that messed up."

".....Huh?"

"I mean, Nara, you just went around being hot. Those sixteen people all changed their faces of their own free will. Everything between you and them is *settled*. It doesn't really matter what any third parties might say or think. Whether they made the right choice, at the very least, you alone should not be getting blamed for it. That's just not fair."

".............!"

Umidori's straightforward rationale hit Nara like a brick, and she gasped aloud.

"U-Umidori…you really did follow every—"

"But not the last part! The last part is totally unacceptable!"

Blowing right past Nara's reaction, Umidori raised her voice to a fiery tone once more.

"Your own mother? One of the few people actually in your corner? I can't believe you went and rejected her! If you don't call her to take that back right now, I don't know what I'll do!"

"……I-I'm so confused," Nara said, clearly lost. "How is that any of your business? So what if I had a fight with my mom? That's our problem.

"A-and she's *not* in my corner. She doesn't understand how I think at all. She's not like me! She's *normal.*"

——*Whap!*

Another hand across her face.

This time, Nara's head was sent spinning in the opposite direction.

"——∿∿∿! Look, do that again, and I'm gonna hit you right back, hear?!"

"Put a lid on it, dumbass! Stop giving me this mealymouthed horseshit!" Umidori was positively huffing and puffing. "S-so this is what *seeing red* means? My hand moved before I knew it! Nara, seriously, you've got your head on totally backward and aren't seeing the forest for the trees!"

"…………?"

"She doesn't understand you at all? She's 'normal'? What are you talking about? That's what's good about her!"

"………Huh?"

"That's why she matters! Don't you get how precious that is? She can't understand you at all, you have totally different values, but *she's still on your side*? You couldn't buy that for all the money in the world, Nara!"

"…………!"

"You've got someone like that right there with you, but you're acting like you're all alone in the world. '*Oh, woe is me, I'm so lonely.*' When obviously, you should be here eating with your parents, not a total stranger like me!"

"…………"

This diatribe at last got through to Nara, and she gasped, silenced.

She thought back to just what her mother said to her in the agency corridor.

"*S-still, I mean it, Yoshino. You may have your eccentricities, but we both love you more than anyone else! That one thing is absolutely true!*"

"——! S-stop it! Stay out of this, Umidori!"

Nara's voice went up, like she was trying to drown out the ripples within.

"I've gotta sit here listening to you run your mouth when you don't know the first thing about us! How could someone like you even begin to understand how I've suffered—"

"Oh, I get it."

"..............You do?"

"I know all too well how you feel, Nara. I'm the same."

".........How's that work?"

"I'm not exactly normal, either," Umidori said, her voice falling. "I was born with a kind of curse. No matter how I try, I just can't live like ordinary people do."

".........A curse?"

"And because of that curse, I've had one bad experience after another. So at the least, I do know how hard being different is, Nara."

"......??"

"But I can say this for a fact. I've *never* had anyone on my side. I don't have *anyone* like your parents."

Umidori was less complaining than persuading.

"I really envy the fact that you have them. And I think it's a real waste to push them away."

"..............."

"Pick up your phone, Nara. All you've gotta do is say sorry. If you don't do that now, I think you'll regret it the rest of your life."

"...................."

Nara lowered her eyes, thinking this over.

Honestly, the last bit didn't make much sense to her, but Umidori had a point—Nara's mother had come running over out of pure concern, and the way she'd treated her might have been out of line. Worse, if she kept balking at making this call, the girl across from her would probably punch her. (Nara was very sure of this.) And a fistfight really *would* leave a permanent scar. She had to avoid that outcome at all costs.

"……Fine!" she said at last. "I'll call her. Satisfied?"

Nara took her phone out of her skirt pocket.

She pulled up her contacts, found her mother's number, tapped the dial button, and held it to her ear. She heard it ringing. At last, it picked up, and Nara said, "Oh, hello? It's Yoshino, is now a good—"

"Wahhhhhhhhhhhhhhhhhhhh!"

——Before she could even finish, an unearthly shriek echoed from the speaker, drowning out her words.

"——?! Uh, M-Mom? What's wrong?"

"……Augh, Yoshinooo!"

At least words emerged, through the sobs.

"I-I'm so sorry!"

"Um……?"

"I was so out of line! I made you sad again!"

"………………Huh?"

"Y-you're always trying to get us to understand, but I'm so dumb I can't make head nor tails of it. I'm a terrible mother! I'm sorry! I'm so sorry, Yoshino……!"

The remorse was so palpable it took Nara quite a while to respond.

She couldn't comprehend what her mother was saying, much less why she was apologizing.

This call was meant to be Nara's apology.

"……! D-don't, Mom! Stop apologizing! No more crying! I was clearly the one in the wrong there! One hundred percent!"

A stabbing pain in Nara's chest almost made her face twist (almost—it didn't actually budge) and she began desperately trying to settle her mother down.

"You were worried about me and came running, and I acted like a spoiled brat. I should be apologizing to you."

"……*Sniff!* No, that doesn't matter now, Yoshino. You said you didn't need dinner—did you already eat out somewhere?"

"……Um."

"Just…if you feel up to it…" At that point, Nara's mom hesitated. "I've actually got all the ingredients for *okonomiyaki* on hand…"

"——!"

"I mean, that's your favorite. Today was a big day, so I thought you'd want some... Dad hasn't eaten yet, either, so if you come home now, we can all eat together!"

"............"

Nara could not have been more stiff if she'd been struck by lightning.

Before her eyes were the remains of some *modanyaki*. Already eaten.

Given how Nara normally ate, this would be more than enough for one meal.

She stared at it for several seconds in silence.

Then she said, "Mm, okay. Thanks, Mom. I haven't eaten yet, so I'll come right home."

Despite the long silence before she answered, her voice betrayed no further hesitation.

They exchanged a few more words, then hung up. With a long sigh, she turned back to Umidori.

"Well? Good enough for you, Umidori?"

"............"

But Umidori didn't respond.

She was sound asleep.

Face down on the counter, snoring away.

"Hah?! You fell asleep?! What the—?!"

Nara was utterly baffled. All that anger, forcing her to call, and now this?!

"......Still, I guess I really owe you one."

She let out a poker-faced sigh, then poked Umidori in the cheek.

"Thanks, Umidori. If I'd missed out eating Mom's *okonomiyaki* tonight, I really would have regretted that the rest of my life. I promise I'll pay you back for this someday."

The next day, Umidori came to school nursing a nasty headache, with no memories of any of this.

——But Nara would remember what Tougetsu Umidori had done for her the rest of her life.

◇◇◇◇

Even once the fallicide was complete, Nara showed no signs of pulling away from Umidori.

Bullshit-chan eating Hurt meant every change brought about by her power was now a lie. Umidori's wounds, the victims left hospitalized by her prior attacks, even the door to Umidori's apartment—everything went back to the way it had been. Umidori insisted there was no more cause for alarm, but Nara wasn't buying it.

"Nope, nope, nope! I'm not going anywhere! You can't push me away! Until I'm absolutely certain you're safe, the anxiety would eat me alive! I'm staying with you all day!"

Like Bullshit-chan, Nara had agreed to Umidori's reckless plan in the spur of the moment, but in hindsight, she really regretted that decision. She'd been a complete mess. Tears had been streaming down her face as she refused to let go of Umidori's arm, like a child clinging to their mother.

For lack of better options, Umidori had held her hand tight the whole train ride back to Nara's house. Once they'd gotten there and rang the doorbell, Nara was still loath to let Umidori go; her mother had needed to come out and gently peel her away. Only then was Umidori free.

"I'm thinking we put a pin in murdering Nara's lie for now," Bullshit-chan said.

On the way home, the train to Isuzunomiya Station—the one closest to Umidori's apartment. They were standing, hanging on to the dangling straps.

"......For now?" Umidori said, peeling her eyes off the wrinkles Nara's tears had left in her uniform shirt.

"Yes. But not because Nara and Envy Sakura bailed us out this time," Bullshit-chan said, eyes on the view scrolling past outside the window. "Like I said back in your room, I fully intended to finish off Nara's lie for reasons unrelated to my own survival. Basically, she may not have received Mud Hat's hypnosis—but she seemed just like the Beliars in that faction. I was certain she was a societal evil, and one I could not let roam free.

"But after spending a whole day with her, I've had to correct that assumption. Something about her seems fundamentally different from those liars."

Bullshit-chan sighed.

"That said, through junior high, Nara *was* exactly like them. Yet the second-year high school version of her just seems like a really *nice* girl. This is a fascinating transformation. What got through to her over the last year and change?"

"......Uh, I wouldn't know," Umidori said, her mind boggled.

Why was Bullshit-chan asking her? She had no insights into Nara's mind or how her beliefs may have shifted.

Or at least, she seemed convinced that was the case.

"But well... Like you said, I think we can put a pin in that problem for now," Umidori agreed, eyes on her tear-stained shirt front again. "No matter what happens, Nara is never going to turn against the world at large."

Perhaps a day before, she could not have said that with confidence.

But right now—Umidori believed that with her whole heart.

"After all, she's on *my* side."

◇◇◇◇

Another hour later...

They were back in Umidori's apartment. The door was definitely back to normal.

"Mm, I admit, I was wrong," Umidori said, nodding over some ginger pork. "I can see why you said you're a good cook. I really didn't think it would be *this* good. Proper food!"

"I appreciate it," Bullshit-chan said, miming a florid bow.

They were seated on opposite sides of the round table.

A number of plastic dishes were lined up on top of it. Plates containing ginger pork, rolled eggs, spinach *nibitashi*, salad, miso soup... Bullshit-chan had made every one of these in the brief window since they arrived home.

"They say the ideal meal is three dishes with rice and soup on the side. But none of this is fancy enough to be worth calling *proper food*, Umidori. It's all stuff you can whip up in a jiffy. To my mind, it's more like I just threw the meal together."

She was being all modest, but she was also clearly tickled pink.

"I'd originally planned to cook something far more impressive. Like three times as involved as what I ended up making. If I get another chance, I'll definitely deliver."

"......Huh, honestly, this more than enough for me," Umidori said, rather rattled by her enthusiasm. "That aside—Bullshit-chan, I do have one last question for you."

"......? Ask away."

"Is there really a Beliar out there who can cure my curse?"

She sounded dubious.

"I've been letting that go unchallenged so far, but the more I think about it, the more it sounds like an awfully vague claim. You might know a lot about lies, but I find it hard to believe you could actually pinpoint anyone who's lies are so specifically what I need.

"If you end up going '*Sorry, Umidori! I did everything I could but failed to find a Beliar who can cure you! Toodles!*' and sail out the door, I'll have to hit you."

"......Yeah, I guess in your position, that'd be the biggest concern." Bullshit-chan nodded. "I mean, the only reason you're helping me is because you want to learn how to lie."

"......Yeah, basically."

"*So I want you think long and hard on it, Umidori. Do you want to save Bullshit-chan? Or should we let her go?*"

When Nara had put that question to her, a whole bunch of stuff ran through Umidori's mind.

The events of the day, her life to that point, the risks of facing Hurt, the threat to her own life...

After chewing all that over thoroughly, Tougetsu Umidori had made her choice.

"I really need to lie, Bullshit-chan. That way, I can be friends with Nara," she said, her voice firm. "Without lies, I've got my techniques—I can live a relatively normal life. But if I stick to that, I'll never be able to call her my friend, no matter how much time passes."

That wasn't exclusive to Nara.

Umidori had given up hoping for all kinds of things because she wasn't normal.

But if she could become normal, then—

"I'll do anything if it lets me lie, Bullshit-chan. Fallicide or whatever—I'll be there with you. Although, if possible, I'd prefer to avoid getting any organs crushed again."

"............No need to worry about that, Umidori," Bullshit-chan said, nodding. "If you help me murder lies, you *will* learn to lie. That is a verified fact.

"You see, I already know the Beliar who can cure your curse."

"...............Oh?"

"I'm not searching out an unseen, unknown Beliar without a clue. I just need to get in touch with one I already know. So your 'toodles' fantasy will not come to pass."

Bullshit-chan flashed her an impish grin.

"Umidori, I am intimately familiar with the Beliar who can save you. I know who they are, what lie they told, and what they're doing right this instant."

"........R-really?!"

This declaration left Umidori's face twitching in shock.

"Wh-why didn't you say so?! That's critical information! Who is it?! At least tell me what lie they told!"

"Heh-heh, not so fast, Umidori. This is the one good card I've got to keep you on my side. I can't show my hand that easily."

Umidori had leaned across the table, and Bullshit-chan was waving her down.

"But I will tell you one more thing—they *aren't* part of the Mud Hat Faction. I knew this Beliar way before I ever encountered Mud Hat. Which also means the faction doesn't know this Beliar exists."

"........So the only way I have of getting in touch with them is through you?"

"Precisely. Ah-ha-ha, isn't that nice, Umidori? Now you *have* to help me."

"...............!"

"We'll talk more about that later. It's getting awfully late. Right now, I can only tell you one thing, Umidori."'

She flashed an indomitable grin and held out a hand.

"Put your faith in me. I *will* grant you the ability to lie. Bullshit-chan may only lie, but rest assured, this alone is one hundred percent the truth."

"......! Oh, come on! You can't end things on something that fishy!"

Umidori scowled down at Bullshit-chan's hand, clearly not buying this at all.

"I still don't even get what you mean! If you could only lie, then you'd just be honest, and frankly, you've said a lot of true things!"

She was shaking her head...

——but soon gave up and took the proffered hand.

Tougetsu Umidori can't lie. Bullshit-chan *is* a lie.

Thus, their black-and-white fallicider partnership was born.

AFTERWORD

Hello, everyone! I'm Kaeru Ryouseirui! Thank you so much for reading my book. I've been trying to become a light novelist since high school and am delighted to finally get my shot.

In hindsight, 2020 proved a turning point in my life. At the time, I was a college student trying to get a real job—but on my fiftieth rejection. "I don't care if they're a sweatshop; just let me work!" I even went to a place so desperate they advertised it as an orientation but it turned out to be the final interview stage. They sent me an offer—then retracted it. It was that bad!

The reason the offer got retracted was because I had to repeat a year of college. The place I was going required 124 credits to graduate, but not just *any* old credits. There were lots of complicated rules. Forty credits from group A, and thirty from group B, etc. I didn't really follow that properly, just took classes at random, and with graduation right around the bend, the admins were like, "Normally, you'd have enough credits to graduate, but you took so many credits that don't help you with that, that'll you'll actually need one hundred and thirty-four."

Then Covid hit, and even I started to realize that there was no light at the end of my job-search tunnel. It was time I dug in. "Becoming a light novelist is my only option!" I spent the next year working on that goal as best I could and, by some miracle, landed a prize—which brings us to today. Being realistic and trying to get a job didn't actually improve my reality, but fleeing from reality actually did change things—isn't life strange?

Now for the thank yous. Editors—I'm so sorry revisions took us nine whole months.

Natsuki Amashiro, I am so, so, so, so sorry for all the scheduling problems I wound up causing you. Yet on a hundred-point cuteness scale, you delivered characters who are eight thousand—and Nara in particular hits sixteen thousand! Thank you so much!

This book had a ton of issues when I submitted it, but the judges saw through that and awarded it the grand prize. I'm ever so grateful. I intend to do everything in my power to live up to your expectations.

That's all I've got. Goodbye! I hope we'll meet again!